"Want to stay he

Her fingers stilled a
"I—I don't think so."

"Why not?"

She paused, then allowed her big brown eyes to focus on his. Her voice was an unintentionally sexy growl. "It might be more dangerous for me here."

"I could sleep on the couch."

"But we both know you wouldn't."

They stared at each other. She was right and Jake did know it. He didn't really give a damn, though. It was inevitable, wasn't it? From the day he'd heard her voice, he'd known what the outcome would be. Known what he wanted it to be.

She rose slowly. "Could you just give me a ride home? I think that'd be the smartest thing." He stood too, his gaze locking on hers from across the room.

"Do you always do the smartest thing?"

Her mouth parted slightly and she took a deep breath. He could see her chest rise and fall beneath her T-shirt.

"Not always, but in this case I think I'd better. Don't you?"

Dear Reader

I travel frequently in my personal life, and as a result often find myself stuck in airports. The idea for *Too Hot for Comfort* came to me in just such a situation. Last year, while sitting in a bar in the Miami International Airport, waiting for a midnight flight to Bolivia, I was idly watching a television talk show and wishing I was somewhere else. And then it struck me.

How do these talk show hosts on TV and radio handle the weird and wacky calls they must get? Larry King never gets flustered…Jerry Springer can handle anything…Oprah always has an answer. How do they do it?

By the time my flight was called, I had my notebook in hand and half this story plotted. Somewhere over Central America my characters came to life and began to fall in love. By the time we flew over Bogota, Sally and Jake knew their love was doomed. Hearts always triumph, however, and touching down in Santa Cruz, eight hours later, theirs was a love story—a funny love story—that would prove once and for all that love can be found in the most unexpected places.

I hope you enjoy reading *Too Hot for Comfort* as much as I enjoyed creating it. And next time you call into a talk show, remember Sally…

Best Wishes,

Kay David

TOO HOT FOR COMFORT

BY

KAY DAVID

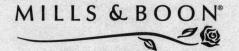

MILLS & BOON®

To my wonderful husband, Pieter. I love you.

First published in Great Britain 2002
Harlequin Mills & Boon Limited,
Eton House, 18-24 Paradise Road, Richmond, Surrey TW9 1SR

© Carla Luan 2000

ISBN 0 263 82934 0

Set in Times Roman 10½ on 12½ pt.
01-0502-38316

Printed and bound in Spain
by Litografia Rosés, S.A., Barcelona

1

"Go ahead, caller. You're on the air!"

"I...I—well, I've never done this kind of thing before. Called in to a radio show. I'm kinda nervous."

"That's all right. We're all friends here at KHRD. What's your question?"

"Well, um... I—I don't exactly know how to put it."

Sally Beaumont grinned at the woman standing beside her, Linda Javin, her best friend and co-producer. They were in the soundproof engineer's room next to the broadcast booth and they could see Mary Margaret Henley from where they stood as she spoke into the mike. Mary Margaret had come to the station dressed for her part—a radio star. She wore a fake Chanel suit she'd gotten in Dallas and full makeup, including her favorite shade of lavender eye shadow. She'd informed Sally and Linda right off the bat that it made her eyes look like Elizabeth Taylor's. Her hair was sprayed and teased until it could have stood up and walked out of the booth on its own had it not been anchored so firmly to Mary Margaret's head by an enormous set of headphones.

"You go ahead now, caller. We all want to hear your question."

Caller sounded like "collar" and *hear* had come out as "here a." Mary Margaret had more than a Texas accent. She had a *west* Texas accent and no word had only one syllable, no matter how it was spelled. Her intonation had given Sally pause but in the end, she'd decided it didn't really matter. Mary Margaret was known for miles. She was the best cook this side of Amarillo and Sally had been thrilled to snag the woman for her latest brain-child—a call-in talk show about cooking.

Too Hot for Comfort was bound to be a hit—the women of Comfort, Texas, had little to do during the blistering summer months besides cook, clean house, and corral their children who had been freed from school. They kept the radio blaring the whole blessed day so the audience was a built-in one for sure.

It was going to be the hit that got Sally out of town.

Mary Margaret glanced toward Linda and Sally and smiled royally as she spoke into the micro-phone. "We've all been 'round the kitchen more than once here, honey, you just go on ahead and ask your question. Don't be shy.''

Encouraged by the familiar and friendly voice, the caller spoke again, this time in a rush. ''Well, you see, my husband wants to do something I'm not real sure about.'' She dropped her voice. ''Something naughty. It kinda sounds like fun…but I've haven't let anyone spank me since I was five years old. He says he wants to be my sugar daddy and make me his honey bunny.'' She giggled. ''What do you think? Should we try it?''

Linda gasped loudly while Sally stared dumbly through the glass. Mary Margaret sat perfectly still, her face a frozen mask. The caller couldn't have possibly said what Sally thought she'd said, so why didn't Mary Margaret answer her? Why didn't she tell her how to whip egg whites into a frothy cloud? Why didn't she explain the difference between chop and mince?

The caller spoke again, and this time she sounded more assured than she had at first, almost chatty. ''Well, I told him I wouldn't wear the diaper—no way—but I might not mind the other if I got to return the favor, you know what I mean?''

Silence. Utter, total silence.

From a primitive level devoted to survival, Sally's brain issued a call to arms, and she jumped in front of the window to gesture wildly at Mary

Margaret. "Answer her, for God's sake," Sally screamed. "Say something. Say anything!" But the woman had gone deaf, dumb *and* blind. She ignored Sally's wild gyrations and sat paralyzed with some emotion Sally could only guess at.

"You better get in there and resuscitate her." Linda shot Sally a frantic look. "I think she's died and gone to cooking heaven."

Mary Margaret's tinted cheeks *were* white and her eyes had begun to roll back in her head. It took Sally only a moment to decide what to do. She couldn't embarrass the caller and tell her she'd mistaken a cooking show for a sex show. The explanation would only make things worse. She had to get the woman off the phone as soon as possible and that meant only one thing: answering her. Sally grabbed the microphone in the engineering booth and spoke, her voice more composed and self-assured than she expected, her heart pounding inside her chest. "Well, caller, if this is something you both want to try and no one's going to get hurt by it, why not? I say spank and let spank!"

The woman on the phone let loose an audible breath. "Really? You—you don't think this is too weird?"

Weird? Everything in Comfort was weird and Sally ought to know. She had lived there her whole life, except for four years—four glorious years—in Houston when she'd attended the university there.

"I think you're really cooking!" she choked out. "Thanks so much for calling and now we're going to hear from our sponsor—"

With her pulse thundering, she punched the kill button, cued up a commercial for Johnny's LP and Feed then jerked open the door to the booth. "Mary Margaret! Get a grip! You've got to think on your feet here."

The woman's shaded eyes took in Sally's face as if she were a visitor who'd suddenly dropped in from a different universe. "Did you heah that question? What kind of cookin' question is that?"

"She obviously made a mistake and thought the show was about something else. You have to be prepared for a few nut cases."

"Y-you told me you screened these calls!"

Sally felt her face flame. She and Linda had been so excited they'd forgotten they were supposed to be doing that very thing. "We do but—"

Linda's voice reached the booth with sudden urgency. "Back in ten, Sally!"

Ignoring Linda, Mary Margaret stared accusingly at Sally. "Well, then what kinda screening was that?"

"We—we goofed up, Mary Margaret. I'm sorry. Please—"

"Back in five!"

"Well, I'm not doing this. No siree!" Ripping off the headset, the woman rose from the padded chair, grabbed her handbag and clutched it to her chest. "I don't talk about S.E.X." She spelled out the word, couldn't even say it. "Especially to strangers—*especially* to strangers who want…who want to spank each other!" Full of indignant self-respect, she brushed past Sally in a haze of Jungle Gardenia and fled from the room.

Suddenly speechless, Sally looked toward Linda. She was holding up three fingers and folding them down, a second at a time. With her heart in her throat, Sally raced from the booth at the very last second and punched the tape back in. Johnny's LP was going to get a bonus today. As the commercial started over, Sally stared at her friend in dismay. "This is a disaster!"

"I know." Linda shook her head. "I'm sorry, Sally. I should have been doing my job instead of standing there watching, but good Lord Almighty! What on earth made that woman think the show was about sex?"

"No one knew what it was about!" Sally moaned. "Rita only gave us four thirty-second promos in the past four weeks. It could have been about car repair for all anyone knew."

Linda wore a hopeless expression. "Well, what are we going to do?"

"You're going to get your butt in there and start answering questions."

Both women turned abruptly as Rita March spoke. The station manager was a tall and imposing woman. Very imposing. And very tall. Few people argued when she pronounced something, and none of her employees dared voice anything but agreement. She stared down at Sally with frosty blue eyes and an even chillier demeanor. Sally had two seconds to wonder if she'd heard her complaint about the advertising, then Rita spoke again.

"You lined up five new sponsors for this show and I won't have them listening to dead air. What's *on* the air is bad enough. I can only imagine the phone calls I'm going to be getting. Get in there and fix this."

She knew better, but this was a desperate situation. Sally dared to argue. "Rita—this is a cooking show. I—I don't know how to cook."

"It *was* a cooking show. Now it's a sex show, thanks to that idiot whose bum is going to be red tonight. Turn on that mike and start talking about S.E.X. Tomorrow we'll kill it." The rest of the message went unspoken but it was just as clear. *And you, too…* She added a final zinger. "You *do* know something about sex, don't you?"

Behind them, Linda snickered. Sally sent her a baleful glare. "It's been a while, but I think I can manage it."

"Then you're on. Come to my office as soon as this disaster is over."

With a sinking heart, Sally watched her boss disappear down the hall while behind her Linda spoke again, her voice almost machinelike. "Back in five," she said.

Sally had only one thought.

What would her father say? Lamon Beaumont was the minister of the only Methodist church in town and he would not appreciate this turn of events. No way.

She leapt into the booth and grabbed the headphones just as Linda pointed her finger and mouthed the words "And now!"

"You're on, caller," Sally's mouth was so dry the words seemed to stick inside. She forced them out, remembering the first time in college she'd run a broadcast. *They don't know you're nervous,* her professor had said. *They can't see you. Just talk.* "What's on your mind?"

This time the caller was a man. Sally prayed for a question about garlic or chopped liver or how to boil an egg—anything but sex. God wasn't listening, though.

She hoped her father wasn't, either.

"Well, uh, there's this widow woman who lives down the road from me, and well, uh, we've kissed a time or two and I think she's ready to move on."

"And?"

"Well…do you know anything 'bout them condoms that glow in the dark?"

"SHERIFF, SHERIFF—you just gotta listen to this. You ain't gonna believe it. Turn your radio on."

The woman's voice was high and strident, and Jake Nolte turned immediately, even though she wasn't addressing him. He wasn't the sheriff, he wasn't an officer, he wasn't anything anymore but a retired cop. It was a strange feeling and he still wasn't used to it.

Jake's best friend, Bob MacAroy, who was the sheriff, looked at his dispatcher poised in the doorway. She was what Jake's daddy would have called a "full-figured woman." The two main reasons for that were bouncing up and down beneath the straining buttons of her uniform shirt as she jumped from one foot to the other. She seemed extremely upset, her bright eyes bugging outward, her face a shade of red Jake hadn't seen in a long time. The women he knew back in Houston didn't blush. About anything.

"What *is* it, Darlene? Can't you see I'm in a meeting and—"

''I know, Sheriff, I know.'' She shot an apologetic glance in Jake's direction, her chest heaving, her breath so short she could hardly speak. ''I'm real sorry, but I think you ought to hear this! It...it's disgraceful! We might need to do something about it—go down to the station or something.''

Bob lifted his hands in a gesture of defeat. Then he swung his chair around to flip on the radio resting on the credenza behind him. He hadn't asked the dispatcher which frequency to tune in and Jake knew why as he remembered where he was. A town the size of Comfort was lucky to have one station much less two. Bob didn't have to ask.

The voice blared out as clearly as if the speaker was in the next room. Bob picked up his coffee and took a sip.

''I'm just awondering about these condom things. I'm not shooting blanks and she's fifty— just a young 'un still. I wouldn't want anything happening here, but I'm not crazy about putting something between me and her. I like to really feel my women, ya know?''

The swallow of coffee Bob had just taken spurted out in an arch across his desk and landed wetly on a stack of neatly typed reports. Darlene wasn't going to like *that,* Jake thought idly. Bob started to laugh. "Shit-fire! That's Elmer Holley, down at the gas station! What the hell…?"

Darlene's mouth pursed into a tiny circle. "Sheriff! Watch your mouth. There's a lady present, don't ya know?"

"I know, Darlene, I know, and I am very sorry. Please forgive me. It's just that…" He glanced toward Jake then back at the radio. "I—I can't believe old Elmer—"

"Shh—" She tilted her head. "Listen to this."

The woman's voice that answered was rich and lush with an unconventional gravelly tone to it. Full of self-assuredness and definitely in control, the voice made Jake think of warm sheets and even warmer bodies. For a second he imagined what she must look like. Curvy, he was sure, with long, silky hair that hung down a slim, elegant back. Her eyes would be smoky, dark with promise.

"You've brought up a really important issue, caller. Condoms aren't just for birth control anymore, and everyone needs to practice safe sex. STDs are everywhere—"

"S T whats?"

"STDs—sexually transmitted diseases— There's some nasty bugs running around these days and even if you haven't been sexually active in awhile—

"In awhile! It's been a coon's age!"

"That doesn't matter. One of the fastest growing segments of the AIDS population is the elderly. You need to protect yourself. Always."

The man spoke again, this time more subdued. "Well, thanks. I—I never thought about that."

"You should," the woman answered. "We all need to, regardless of our age or sexual preferences. Thanks for calling." A slight pause came over the air, then the sexy voice resumed. "This is KHRD, broadcasting from downtown Comfort. You've been listening to *Too Hot For Comfort*." For the first time since she'd begun to speak, she stammered slightly. "This is S-Sally Beaumont saying goodbye for today." Music immediately filled the tiny office as Bob swung his chair around and shook his head.

"Boy, oh, boy. Sally Beaumont! I can't believe it."

"Well, aren't you gonna do something?" Darlene put her hands on her hips. They were well-padded. Her holster would never fall down on its own.

Bob looked at the dispatcher with patient exasperation. Jake had seen the same expression a thousand times when they'd both been cops back in Houston, on the street as partners. "Haven't you heard of the First Amendment, Darlene? The right to free speech?"

"But that's pornography!"

Bob's brown eyes went flat and dark and Jake knew what was coming. Darlene had stepped over the line.

"No. *That is not pornography.*" Bob spoke each word slowly and distinctly, as if to make sure she got his point. "Now, if you don't mind, I'd like to finish my conversation with the lieutenant, here. Please shut the door and don't disturb us any more."

With an audible huff, the woman closed the door. Jake looked at Bob and spoke for the very first time, saying only one word. "Pornography?"

Bob shrugged, a disgusted frown now marring his forehead. "It's a conservative town, Jake. What can I say? Darlene's not alone. This is going to raise some eyebrows, that's for sure. I never would have thought little Sally Beaumont would do something like that…"

Jake thought of the voice. The sexy, dark voice. His image didn't match with someone Bob would refer to as "little" Sally Beaumont. His curiosity got the better of him. "Why is that?"

"Well for one thing, her daddy's the local preacher. They live in town but Sally lives out by the lake—'bout five minutes from my place, as a matter of fact. I wouldn't think of Sally as an expert at sex. She was a good girl back in school."

Jake raised his eyebrows. "A good girl, huh? Guess that means you tried and she turned you down?"

Bob looked indignant. "She's younger than us, for God's sake. A lot younger. Twenty-something."

Jake kept his face neutral. Twenty-something might sound too young for Bob—he'd been married fifteen years to the same woman—but to Jake it sounded just right. Women that young weren't interested in commitments. They liked excitement, entertainment. If he'd been interested, which he wasn't, he might have considered looking into the body that went with the voice. He wasn't interested, though. Not one bit.

"Besides, this is the Bible Belt, Jake, remember? Folks around here don't talk about stuff like that."

Jake started to point out that some of them obviously did, but instead he just shook his head. "It's been a while since I've been here, guess I forgot." His fingers tightened on the scarred wooden arms of the chair where he sat as second thoughts assailed him. "You know, Bob, this might not be such a good place for me after all. I'm not the kind of guy who's gonna fit into a town like this—"

"Not fit in? Hell, you'd fit in anywhere so don't give me that garbage, Nolte. Besides, where else would you go? What else would you do? My cabin out at the lake's been empty for months and you've got to land somewhere. At least until you decide what else you want to do.''

Decide what else he wanted to do? There wasn't a decision to be made. As if his body were agreeing, a vague pain began to ache up and down Jake's right leg. His fingers went automatically to the small indented knot on his upper thigh. A few inches higher and to the left and he wouldn't have had to worry about Elmer's problem ever again. Or any other problem, for that matter. The drug dealer's shot had missed Jake's femoral artery, but barely. Tired of his job and his life, he'd left Houston. Now he wanted to do exactly…nothing.

He realized Bob was speaking again. ''—and Debbie has some friends she wants to introduce you to. They're nice women. You'll have a good time—''

Jake rose slowly. ''I didn't come here for a good time, Bob.''

''Well, I know that, buddy, but it wouldn't kill you to go out some night with us, now, would it? Make some friends, drink some beer, relax a little?''

Jake reached for the keys to Bob's cabin he'd laid on the desk when Jake had first come in. ''It wouldn't kill me,'' he agreed, ''but making friends isn't why I came to Comfort. I want peace and quiet. I want to fish and mind my own business. I

want to get the big city out of my system, Bob.''
He stared down at his old friend. ''Peace and quiet,
buddy. That's all I want.''

SALLY CRAWLED from the broadcast booth down
the hall to Rita's office. At least it felt as if she
were crawling. Her shoulders couldn't have gotten
any lower or her ego, either. *Too Hot for Comfort*
was going to sink her. It *had* been a good idea, she
told herself. It really had. Obviously she should
have picked another name—Cooking in Comfort or
In the Kitchen in Comfort. Anything that would
have made it more clear it was a *cooking* show.
The setup had been great, though, regardless. The
concept *could* have worked. It *could* have gotten
her noticed.

All Sally had ever wanted to do was get out of
Comfort. From the moment she'd returned after college, that had been her single thought. Looking
back on the situation, she wondered where her brain
had been when she'd accepted the job at KHRD.
Sure, times had been tough and jobs in radio or
television had been almost nonexistent, but she
could have looked some more.

She passed the coffeepot and the two ad men,
Sonny LaBouef and Frank Francis, who never left
its side. They eyed her as she walked by and began
to snigger. When she was almost at the end of the

hall, Sonny called out. "Hey, Sal—I got me a date tonight with a girl who has some handcuffs. Should I take her a whip and chain or some flowers?"

Frank, the straight man, cracked up at Sonny's erudite humor.

Sally ignored them both, remembering instead the look on her parents' faces six years ago when she'd told them about the job offer—right there in Comfort. They'd been so proud, so happy. She'd felt the weight of their smiles, and every time she'd considered turning down the position to go farther afield, all she could think of was their resulting disappointment if she'd said no. She was their only child and ever since she'd been old enough to understand what that meant, she'd carried the responsibility of their happiness on her shoulders.

And now here she was, six years later. She hadn't moved on, she hadn't married, she hadn't done a thing. All of her old friends had families of their own—children, dogs, gardens. The ones who didn't sent her E-mail from exotic places like New York and Los Angeles where they had fabulous jobs and wore designer clothing. All she had was a piddling little job at a dying radio station and now she was going to lose that.

Squaring her shoulders the best she could, she opened the door to Rita's office and went inside.

2

RITA'S SECRETARY, Tiffany Jackson, looked up as Sally came into the office. The woman didn't say a word. She didn't have to. Her tight, prissy look said it all. *I'm happy as hell you're about to get fired.*

In the twelfth grade, Ross Martin had asked Sally to the prom instead of Tiffany, and she'd never forgiven Sally for this transgression. Sally told herself she should feel sorry for her if this was all Tiffany had to worry about, but charity came hard when she continually made life difficult for Sally.

"Rita's busy. You'll have to wait." Tiffany's voice was as satisfied as her expression.

Sally nodded and sat down on the couch near the door. After a few minutes, she felt the bottle-blonde's stare, but refused to look at her.

After another five minutes, Sally couldn't stand it any longer. She raised her eyes and met Tiffany's gaze. There was something besides her usual smugness in her glare, but Sally wasn't too sure what it was. For one long moment they stared at each other, then Tiffany spoke.

"How come you know so much about sex?"

Speechlessly, Sally looked at the secretary. "Wh—what?"

"You answered all those questions everyone had and you never even stumbled. I was listening." She narrowed her eyes. "You learn all that stuff while you lived in Houston or did you know it before then?"

...like in the twelfth grade? If she hadn't been about to lose her job, Sally would have laughed out loud. Here was the answer Tiffany had been searching for since high school; *this* was why Ross Martin had picked Sally instead of Tiffany. All those years ago, Sally had obviously known the *Kama Sutra* and where to buy sparkly condoms.

Before Sally could answer, the door to Rita's office came open. She stood in the opening, filling it up, and looked at Sally. "Let's get this over with," she said ominously.

Sally jumped up and followed her boss into her office, closing the door behind her.

"Sit down."

Sally did so gratefully. Her knees were rubbery and her stomach was fighting the jelly doughnut she'd eaten to celebrate the morning's show. Obviously consumed before the show had begun.

Instead of saying anything, Rita went to the wide tinted window behind her desk. She stood there, with her back to Sally, and stared out without saying a word.

Her beige suit blended in with the dusty landscape outside the glass. Summer had just begun, but the heat had been with them for a good month. The parking lot shimmered in the hot Texas sun and little waves of glimmering light rippled across the surface for as far as Sally could see. Beyond the baking cars and steaming asphalt, the pin oaks already looked parched and worn. In the planter beside the window, the lantana had tried to stay perky, but the pink blossoms wore an air of defeat.

Sally felt the same way.

Rita turned around slowly and looked at her. Her question was the last one Sally expected. "You got some pretty strange questions out there. How *did* you know all those answers?"

"They weren't that weird," Sally answered without thinking. "At least not to me. I worked a teen hot line when I lived in Houston, and before I could start taking calls, I had to go through sixty hours of training. Ninety-nine percent of the questions were about sex. It's mostly common-sense stuff anyway."

Rita nodded slowly. "But you didn't get rattled.

You handled yourself well at the mike. Why did you go the producer route?''

"I like the behind-the-scenes work." Sally paused, the words still stinging as she remembered them. "And one of my professors said my voice sounded like rocks being shook up in a bag. He said it'd never work on the air."

Rita raised her eyebrows then walked around the edge of her desk and sat down in one of the chairs beside Sally. "Well, he was wrong. Your voice is wonderful. It's unique and sexy. It's perfect, as a matter of fact."

Sally stared at her dumbly. Personally, she'd never thought there was anything wrong with her voice, but she'd had no desire to be the star, unlike most of her classmates. She'd wanted to get into the nitty-gritty. Plan what the station did. Run the place. But a "perfect" voice? Perfect for what?

"Perfect for what?" she asked.

"Perfect for a show about sex."

Sally thought of Mary Margaret. She knew now how the woman had felt. Stunned. Unable to move. "Wh—what do you mean?"

"I mean the phones have been going crazy since the show was aired—''

"I'll just bet they have—''

Rita shook her head. "It was neck and neck—positive and negative. And we only lost one spon-

sor. The others loved it, especially Johnny's LP.''
She leaned closer to where Sally sat. ''The nega-
tives don't matter, Sally. We got calls, don't you
see? People were listening. They'll be talking about
this for days. They'll be talking…and they'll be listening.''

Sally shook her head. ''I—I don't think I understand, Rita.''

''You have a hit on your hands, girl. A major
hit.''

''But…but this is a cooking show… And Mary
Margaret ran out of here—''

''Forget cooking and forget Mary Margaret. *Too
Hot for Comfort* is no longer about cooking. It's all
about sex and you're going to handle it personally.''

Sally was shaking her head before Rita could finish. ''I don't think…''

''There's nothing to think about, Sally. We've
been taking sponsors all morning. Ed's Drug Em-
porium—you can imagine why they want in—and
Lucy's Secrets, too. You know, that lingerie store
out on the highway? Carl Park's Auto Shop, too,
for some strange reason…''

''Rita, I—I can't host a show like that. I'm not
a disc jockey, I don't know how to talk to people.''

''That's ridiculous, of course you do. You proved
it this morning.'' She stared at Sally. ''You obvi-

ously feel comfortable with the topic and you know something about it. What's the problem?''

Sally hesitated, then she spoke quietly. ''My father would die… I can't embarrass him like that.''

Rita leaned back in her chair and put her hands together, the fingertips touching. She didn't say anything for a moment, then finally she spoke. ''You're twenty-eight, Sally. You want to leave Comfort. This show *could* be an opportunity for you to get noticed. Austin, San Antone—they like to think we're hicks out here and maybe we are— but the point is, it only takes one station to hear this, pick it up and play it. Whether they laugh at us or not, we don't give a shit. All we want is for them to buy it…then you're on your way.'' She paused. ''Are you willing to give up the best chance you've had in years to leave here because of your father?''

Her mind in a turmoil, Sally couldn't say no and she couldn't say yes. She couldn't say anything. Rita was telling the truth, but…

Rita leaned forward and reached for a file on the desk, clearly dismissing Sally for the time being. ''You think about it,'' she said quietly. ''The show's supposed to air again two days from now. I'll obviously need an answer before then.''

JAKE GLANCED at the hand-drawn map one more time, then angled his pickup down the dirt road on his right. It was a good thing Bob was the sheriff because he never would have made it as the local cartographer. Comfort wasn't too complicated, though, and once past the outskirts of town, things got even simpler. You went south, you hit Mexico. You went north, you ended up in Oklahoma. Comfort's one and only body of water—Lake Merriweather—was smack in between the two, about twenty miles out of town. Bob's cabin was on the eastern side of the lake and the sunsets were almost as good as the fishing. He'd invited Jake up a lot when they'd still been together on the force in Houston, but Jake had come only once. Sandra didn't like him going somewhere on his weekends off and after she'd left him, he hadn't had the energy or the desire to make the long drive up from Houston.

But now he was here.

He pulled up in front of the small frame house and killed the engine. Immediate and total quiet enveloped him, along with the scent of something he assumed was fresh air off the lake. It'd been so long since he'd smelled anything but smog, diesel and other big-city fumes, he wasn't too sure. As he walked down the gravel path toward the cabin, pine trees brushed at him and a squirrel, perched on a nearby rock, chattered at him.

Ten minutes later he had his stuff stowed in the cabin and his first chilled beer in his hand. Wandering to the back porch, he sat down in the rocker and looked out over the lake, taking a deep draft of the cold beer as he stared out over the pristine blue water.

"This is it," he said out loud. "This is retirement, Nolte. Whaddya do now?"

He waited, but the answer didn't come—only the sunset. He watched the red sphere dip into the lake, extinguishing the light and heat, then he rose and went back inside. Dinner was a ham sandwich and another beer, then he climbed into bed and turned out the light. Sleep came fast and hard, but when the phone rang, the sound brought him into instant awareness. Without even thinking, he reached across the unfamiliar bed, picked up the receiver and growled "Nolte."

"Jake, it's Bob. Got a problem, man."

For half a second, Jake thought he was in Houston, five years past. Bob's phone calls back then had always started just that way, but a moment later, Jake remembered where he was and suddenly the call didn't make any sense. "What's going on?"

"I got two deputies. One's wife is having a baby in Kerrville, and the other one's on a call over in Sisterdale, little town east of here."

Jake glanced at the bedside clock with bleary eyes. "You called me at two in the morning to tell me this?"

"No, I called you at two in the morning to tell you somebody just threw a big-ass rock into Sally Beaumont's living-room window. You're five minutes away. Could you drive over and calm her down? I'll be there as fast as I can."

Jake was already reaching for his pants, the urgency of Bob's voice making him move fast. "I'm on my way," he said. "Just give me some directions."

SHE'D BEEN HALF ASLEEP, half awake when the sound of breaking glass had brought Sally to full awareness. She'd wanted to duck under the bed and tell herself it was a bad dream, but with her heart in her throat, she climbed out, grabbed the baseball bat she kept nearby and tiptoed into the living room.

The huge picture window that faced the lake had been shattered, and the glass that remained in the frame pointed upward with gaping sharp teeth. Bits and pieces of it lay shining brightly on the floor, the moonlight hitting the shards and making them sparkle like diamonds someone had carelessly scattered. In the center of the broken glass was a rock.

And tied to the rock was a piece of paper.

She'd picked it up and untied the string with trembling fingers, knowing already she wasn't about to read a message of good cheer.

Decent people don't listen to smut!

The letters had been printed in a childish scrawl, an obvious attempt to disguise the handwriting. Sally had taken a deep breath and told herself it was nothing. She would have forgotten about it, cleaned up the mess and gone back to bed, but then she'd seen the other side of the missive.

Shut up or we'll quiet you for good.

And that's when she picked up the phone and called the sheriff.

The man standing before her nodded thoughtfully as Sally finished her narrative.

"You weren't hurt?"

Sally looked up at him and tried not to stare, but that was impossible so she just gave up and looked. Jake Nolte was not the most handsome man she'd ever seen, but there was definitely *something* about him. Something that pulled her gaze and refused to let go. The electric blue eyes? No, they were intriguing but that wasn't it. The coal-black hair still a little messy from his sleep? No, it wasn't that, although she wouldn't mind running her fingers through those dark strands....

He bent over to pick up something off the floor and she couldn't help but notice how well his jeans fit. As attractive as he was in that department, his body wasn't what held her gaze, either. As he straightened and she looked at him again, she decided whatever was holding her interest had nothing to do with his physical attributes, but instead was something about his attitude. He'd been around and seen it all; his air was one of weary acceptance that said nothing surprised him.

But underneath he still cared.

She gave herself a mental shake. All this and she'd known the guy less than five minutes? She really was losing it.

"I—I was in bed," she said, finally answering his question. "In the other room."

"Bob said you sounded shook up."

"I was," she confessed. "It's not every day I get a rock through the window…but then again, it's not every day I talk about S.E.X. on the radio."

He looked at her strangely as she spelled out the word. "Sounds like that's what this is about, but are there any other possibilities?"

"Not that I can think of."

"Got any enemies?"

She shook her head.

"No angry ex-husband? No angry ex-boyfriend?"

"No angry ex-anything."

He had picked up the note from the rock with

her eyebrow tweezers and had put it in a plastic bag from her kitchen. He held the bag up now, their eyes meeting over it, his so blue they almost seemed to glow. "This pretty much explains it, but it never hurts to check."

"S—sure," she answered. A little voice in the back of her head was telling her he'd wanted to know if she had a boyfriend, but then logic took over. He was being a cop, that's all. Doing his job, even though it wasn't really his job, as he'd explained when she'd opened her front door.

He walked over to the window and began to examine the broken glass. Then he lifted his gaze to the lake. "Could have come by water." He turned. "Did you hear a boat? See any lights?"

"No. I was pretty much asleep. The breaking glass woke me. By the time I got here, I'm sure they were long gone."

The lean lines of his body were outlined from the light shining in off the porch. He had to be over six feet, with not an ounce of anything but muscle on his frame. She could only imagine what it would be like to be a bad guy and see him looming in front of you. Not fun, she concluded.

Sitting on a nearby chair, she forced herself to concentrate on the real reason he was there. "It's the radio show, I know it is. This town is so small-minded, nothing would surprise me in that department. Their brains don't go past the city-limit sign."

"If you feel that way, why don't you move?"

She looked up at him, those blue eyes capturing her gaze and holding it. "I have family here."

Before he could ask her more, the doorbell rang. She started to get up, but he held out one hand and stopped her. "Let me," he said, his voice deep and authoritative. "You stay here."

She nodded, then as he walked toward the hall-way, she noticed, for the first time, the small bulge in the waistband at the back of his pants. His shirt was not tucked in and she hadn't realized why until this moment. He had a gun.

He put his hand behind him, on the weapon, and looked out the window of her front door. Immediately relaxing, he grinned and turned the handle. "What kind of response time you got down here?" Jake asked. "You'd be fired back in Houston for taking this long."

"Yeah, yeah…"

Hearing Bob MacAroy's voice, Sally rose and came toward the entry just as the sheriff stepped inside and shut the door behind him.

"Hey there, Sally. Sorry for the delay." He glanced at Jake, then back at her. "Hope you don't mind I sent Jake over. I wanted to get someone here as fast as I could. He was close."

Sally let her gaze go to the tall, silent man standing beside Bob. "I didn't mind," she said slowly. "I didn't mind at all."

Bob walked into the living room, glass crunching beneath his feet. He studied the mess as Jake came up behind him and handed him the note. "This was tied to the rock. Miss Beaumont handled it but you might be able to lift some other prints if you're lucky."

The sheriff nodded. "I'll send it off to Austin. It'll take a while, but you never know. Those DPS boys are pretty good."

He turned around and began to ask Sally the same questions Jake had. Somehow it wasn't quite as interesting answering them the second time around…or maybe it wasn't quite as interesting because Bob was asking them now and not Jake. When Bob had told her he was sending Jake Nolte he'd explained they'd been partners in Houston and Jake was staying at his lake house for a while.

She wondered now what was going on. Why was he at Bob's cabin? Was it just a vacation? How long was "a while?" Everyone in town knew how particular Bob was about his fishing cabin. He guarded it as if it held gold instead of old lures and beat-up furniture. They must be close friends.

Bob's voice brought her attention back to the moment. "I called Junior down at the glass and mirror shop but Betty Lou answered and said he couldn't get here till in the morning. Said he was sleeping at his mother's house…she's down with a bad back again and he was staying with her.'' Bob sent a look toward the open window, then his gaze returned to her. ''Would you like to come over to the house? You could sleep in Brittany's room. She's got bunk beds.''

Sally smiled at the offer, then thought twice about Bob's daughter's room. The ten-year-old had made it a shrine to 'N Sync. It'd be easier to sleep at home with a broken window, than to have that band looking down at her as she tried to snooze. ''Thanks, Bob, but I don't think I'll even go back to bed. I appreciate it, though.''

''You sure? You aren't scared?''

''This is Comfort, remember? Somebody's just making their opinion known, that's all.''

''Yeah, but this is a helluva way to do it.''

Footsteps sounded and they both turned to see Jake Nolte reenter the room. ''Maybe you could go stay with your family for a few days,'' he said. ''Until things settle down.''

''No.'' She spoke quickly, without even thinking. ''I don't want to do that. I'll stay here. I'll be fine, I'm sure.''

The blue eyes studied her, then he nodded slowly as if he understood everything she wasn't saying.

That her parents would take her in, but the cost would be her privacy and independence—two things she valued above all. That she didn't want to embarrass her father any more than she already had. That it would just…complicate her life even more.

"Well, I'm down the road if you need me." Jake Nolte ducked his head in Bob's direction, then he walked out the front door without another word.

3

AFTER NAILING UP a piece of plywood over the open window, Bob MacAroy left. By the time Sally got dressed and had her first cup of coffee, the sun was rising over the lake. She stood on her porch, where Jake Nolte had been an hour earlier, and stared out over the water. It was as blue and remote as his eyes and once again, she wondered what kind of man he was. There was something awfully intriguing about him. Immediately she analyzed her reaction—she analyzed everything and planned everything—and she began to question herself. Was it him or just the fact that he wasn't from Comfort? She'd had a few near misses with guys in town—had almost let Max Swinford put a diamond on her hand—but at the last moment she always thought about what it would mean to marry a man from Comfort.

Staying there. Forever.

She swigged down the rest of her coffee, then turned and went inside, the thought bringing her full circle. Rita had told her the show could be her ticket out of here, but as Sally thought about the price, she still wasn't sure she was ready to pay it. She was surprised her parents hadn't called already, but yesterday had been her mother's bridge day and her father had probably been too busy. Summer in Comfort meant only one thing to him—Vacation Bible School. For two weeks, he'd have a church full of kids and nothing else would matter. She'd forgotten about that yesterday during the broadcast, otherwise she wouldn't have been so worried. He never listened to the radio when VBS was about to start. He didn't have the time.

Which might make this morning the perfect opportunity, she thought suddenly. She could go to the house and discuss the show with her mother. Maybe feel her out about it first. She was always the easy one.

Grabbing her briefcase, Sally left the house, locking the door behind her. She passed Bob's cabin five minutes later and turned her head automatically to look down the dusty drive. She caught a quick glimpse of a red pickup truck, but nothing more amid the oaks. If Jake Nolte was human, he'd probably gone back to bed, she surmised. The thought was all her poor brain needed. Instantly the image of the tall cop, tangled in the sheets, shot into her mind. Bare-chested with his hair tousled and his smile inviting…his appearance—even if it was imaginary—made her throat tighten and her heart race. He wouldn't be alone in bed, of course. She would be lying beside him, one leg thrown over his with possessive sensuality. The picture played out, with Sally reaching over for him, her hand trailing over his chest. She shook her head, as if to dispel the vision, but stubbornly it refused to leave. Only after she parked in her parents' driveway, did the fantasy finally disappear.

REBECCA BEAUMONT met her daughter on the doorstep of the house where Sally had grown up. She held a pink mixing bowl with a plastic spoon sticking out of it, and in the bright Texas sun, her mother's white hair gleamed. "I was in the kitchen when I saw you pull in the driveway," Rebecca said with a smile. "What a treat! You almost never visit before work!" She held up the bowl. "I'm making French toast. Want some?"

Sally's mouth watered, then she thought again. "Is Dad here?" she said cautiously.

"No, no. He's left already. I got hungry and thought 'why not?' I can fix French toast just for me, can't I?"

Sally smiled and nodded, more relief than she'd expected flooding her. "French toast sounds great. I'll share it with you."

They stepped into the cool dim hallway, heading

for the kitchen, Rebecca chattering all the way. Sally let her talk, but through the effervescence she thought she sensed a nervous thread, unusual for her mother. By the time the toast was ready and they'd sat down at the table, Sally was sure Rebecca *had* heard the broadcast—but she was waiting for Sally to speak first.

The bite of crispy toast and sweet maple syrup Sally had just taken turned to dust in her mouth. Swallowing painfully, she put down her fork and faced her mother. "Mom, I came by for a reason this morning. I—I wanted to know if you heard the—"

"I heard the show," her mother said. "Dorothy called and canceled bridge yesterday because her shingles were acting up so I stayed home." Rebecca Beaumont placed her own fork down on the pristine white place mat beneath her plate. Her voice and features stayed neutral. "I heard it all."

Sally sat nervously, her stomach churning. "Did Daddy?"

"No. He didn't actually hear it. I—I told him about it and I'm sure he'll learn more today."

Sally didn't need more explanation; she knew what her mother was talking about. The Comfort phone lines were probably smoking, they were so busy.

Sally waited for her mother to say more, but she

didn't. What thoughts were running through her head? How to tell Sally she'd been disowned? How to tell her what a disappointment she was?

Finally Rebecca spoke, a delicate pink blush staining her soft cheeks as the words began. "Sally, sweetheart, I—I was wondering…not that I need any or anything but…do condoms really come with sparkles now?"

Sally stared at her mother. In the background of her mind, she heard music. It sounded like the theme from *The Twilight Zone*.

"Sally?"

"Uh, yeah…I'm here."

Her mother stared at her expectantly. "Well?"

"Um, yes, Mom, they do. With sparkles and glitter and ribs and everything else you can imagine—and some things you can't." Before she could say more, her mother spoke again.

"And that other woman—the one who wanted her boyfriend to tie her up? Do a lot of young folks go in for that sort of thing?"

The conversation was taking such an unreal air that Sally imagined herself floating up from the chair and looking down on the two of them from the white plastic light fixture her father had installed when she'd been in the fifth grade. Unbelievably, her mother didn't appear upset, only curious. What was going on? What alien had taken over her mother's body?

"Do they use that yellow kind of rope you get down at the hardware store or do they use something special?"

"You—you can use anything you like," Sally said without thinking, her brain spinning. "Velvet rope, scarves, chains... I don't think there's too many rules as far as bondage is concerned."

"Bondage...hmmm."

Just hearing the word come from her mother's lips was too much. Sally stood up abruptly and took her plate to the kitchen sink. What was happening? Why was her mother asking these questions instead of telling Sally how she'd ruined their lives? Taking a deep breath, Sally turned and faced her mother. "The program—it—it didn't upset you?"

Rebecca looked surprised. "Upset me? Heavens no. I wasn't upset, honey. Why should I be? Sex education is a wonderful thing and for a lot of years your father has been considering just such a thing at the church. He simply didn't know what to do or how to do it. I think your program is wonderfully educational. We're proud of you. Really we are!"

Sally's mouth actually fell open. Her mother's words were so unexpected, she couldn't control herself. "Are you crazy? You think it's an educational program?"

Her mother nodded solemnly. "Well, of course, darling. What else could it be? People have questions. They need answers. We know you worked on the hot line in college. This is just the same only it's being broadcast. You're helping many more people."

"And this is how Daddy feels, too?"

"Well…yes. He was a little concerned at first, but after I explained it to him, he understood. How hard you'd worked on the program and how much you wanted to help people. How you felt it would be good for your career. After that, he wasn't upset."

"How much I wanted to help people! Mom! You knew that show was supposed to be about cooking, not sex!"

"Oh, I don't think so." Rebecca spoke slowly, her gaze meeting Sally's from across the kitchen, the lingering homey smell of French toast in the air between them. "I distinctly remember you telling me something quite different—and once I explained that to your father, he wasn't upset at all."

Stunned, Sally gripped the edge of the sink and stared at her mother. She didn't understand. She'd expected her mother to be horrified and her father clutching his chest. Instead, Rebecca Beaumont was helping her daughter, actually paving the way and smoothing things over with her father before they'd

even had a chance to get rough. "A-are you sure?"
*Are you sure this is okay and neither of you are
going to get hurt?*

"Absolutely." Rebecca Beaumont met her
daughter's startled and confused gaze without hes-
itation, a steady thoughtful look on her face that
contained a message that went beyond the words
she spoke. "I think *Too Hot For Comfort* is a public service this town has needed for a very long
time. We're proud of you, Sally. Very proud." Suddenly her eyes began to twinkle. "In fact, I can't
wait to hear the next installment."

AFTER REACHING WORK, Sally suffered the jokes
and snide remarks everyone on staff seemed determined to make at her expense. She got more than
one or two ugly looks, as well. The receptionist,
Loretta Smith, a blue-rinsed member of Sally's father's church, leaned over at the coffee machine and
whispered, "How could you? Your poor father..."
Loretta's best friend at the station, Pearl Westbrook
down in typing, echoed Loretta's sentiments. At the
lunch counter, she made a point of bringing her tray
to Sally's table and then turning on her heel to walk
in the other direction. It would have been funny...if
Sally hadn't gotten a rock through her window at
2:00 a.m.

Linda could hardly believe it when Sally told her

about the rock and the message. "Who would do something like that?"

"Who knows?" Sally answered, shaking her head. She pushed a fork through the salad she'd selected, feeling so confused she hardly knew which end was up. She'd been totally prepared for her parent's reproach, but they were supporting her. What was going on? And then there was Jake Nolte. At the oddest moments he kept popping into her head. She told Linda about his and Bob's arrival last night.

"Whoa, whoa…" Linda held up one hand. "Jake Nolte. Is he the hunk staying out at Bob's place?"

Sally looked at her in amazement. "You know him?"

"Not really, but Debbie told me he was coming. She said she might try and fix me up with him." Linda leaned closer. "What do you think? Should I go for it?"

Something that felt curiously like jealousy poked Sally in the ribs. "I don't know," she said stiffly. "He seems rather remote to me."

Linda stared at her for a few seconds then burst out laughing, her eyes twinkling. "*Raather remote?* Oh, baby! You've already got your little paws out for him, don't you?"

"That's not true!"

"Oh, puleeze…. You're so easy to get a rise out of, it's hardly even fun." Linda leaned over the table. "If you like the guy, tell Debbie. The only reason she didn't ask you in the first place is that you never seem interested, Sally. You've turned down everyone's attempts to match you up with someone."

"I'm usually *not* interested," she said, toying with a piece of lettuce. Looking up, she grinned, "But I might be willing to make an exception this time."

Linda rolled her eyes. "Then call her, for God's sake. They're having a barbecue out there at the camp on Saturday." She started to say more, but suddenly fell silent. Sally looked up in time to see Rita approaching. The station manager stopped at their table and stared at Sally.

"I understand you had some problems out at your place last night."

Sally nodded. She wasn't surprised Rita knew.

"If your insurance won't cover it, the station will pay for the glass. I've already told Bubba to send us the bill." She leaned down. "This should make your decision a little easier."

"What do you mean?"

"If you don't go back on the air, they win." Rita's eyes were like flint. "This is your chance to prove what you're worth, Sally. Don't let some idiot with a rock make up your mind for you. I'll expect you in my office tomorrow morning, giving me the answer I want to hear.'' Her steely gaze pierced Sally's a second longer, then she turned around and walked away.

Watching the station manager leave, Linda and Sally sat in silence. Linda spoke only after Rita disappeared through the lunchroom doors. ''I wonder what she paid him?''

Sally frowned. ''Paid who?''

Linda smiled. ''The guy with the rock.''

JAKE ANGLED HIS pickup truck into the parking spot directly in front of Brookshire Brother's Groceries. When he'd arrived in town last night, he'd only bought the necessities—cold beer, frozen pizzas, sandwich stuff—but now he was going to have to do some major shopping. More beer, of course, a pound of hamburger and maybe some eggs. And another few pizzas, too. He climbed from the truck and made his way into the store, his eye on a dark-headed woman in front of him. For a second, he thought it was Sally Beaumont, then he realized his mistake when the woman turned. Sally was much slimmer and wore her hair smooth and short. Last night, he'd watched the silky brown curtain swing against her neck as she'd answered his questions;

every so often she had tucked it behind her ears with slim, pale fingers.

He grabbed a cart from a jumbled line and pushed it into the fruit section with more vigor than necessary. Sally Beaumont hadn't been at all what he'd expected. When she'd opened the door to her house, he'd been more than surprised. Her voice definitely didn't match the rest of her. The curves he'd imagined were more gentle than voluptuous; the sexy, smoldering eyes he'd conjured had turned out to be brown—soft and huge with lashes so long they brushed her cheeks when she lowered her eyes. She'd looked innocent and naive. It was hard to reconcile that gravelly, sexy voice with the slim young woman who'd greeted him.

He threw a couple of tomatoes in the cart and pushed it down the next aisle. What in the hell was he doing thinking of Sally Beaumont anyway? She was young—a career woman concerned with nothing but her job. There was no ''ex-anything'' she'd told him, and to back up her point, her house had contained no photos of her with friends, no outward signs of any hobby, nothing to show that she thought of anything but work. The magazines on her coffee table had been trade journals and the books reference guides. No novels for Sally Beaumont. No novels and no old boyfriends.

He reached the end of the second aisle without

picking up a thing. Sally still on his mind, he headed to the dairy counter for the eggs, barely missing an old lady with two bags of cat food in her arms. He hadn't been interested in a woman since Sandra had left him, their divorce a cold and short-lived contest. She'd been a career woman, too. A mortgage banker. They'd met in a cop bar and had gotten married six weeks later. He didn't really know why, except the sex had been great. Everything else had been the pits. After five miserable years, they'd gone their separate ways.

Thinking of Sandra was like stepping into a cold shower. All thoughts of dating anyone else, including Sally, went out the window. Jake finished his shopping, went through the checkout, grabbed up the white plastic bags and headed outside.

Sally Beaumont was leaning against the fender of his pickup.

WHEN JAKE CAME OUT of Brookshire Brothers carrying his groceries, Sally's breath caught in her throat and a funny twist of something warm started in her stomach. *Whoa there, girl. Slow down, take it easy!* The words of warning sounded inside her head but her body wasn't listening. Actually, the rest of her hadn't listened too well, either. When she'd seen the shiny red pickup, her brain had ordered her to keep going, but her hands had turned the steering wheel and swung her car into the asphalt lot to park. Then her fingers had unlocked the door, her legs had jumped out, and here she was, leaning against his vehicle, her heart doing a rhumba.

His blue eyes seemed to warm as they took her in, but it could have just been her imagination. "Hi, there." His voice was deep and sexy.

"Hi, yourself," she answered. She nodded to the grocery bags, seeing the beer through the plastic. "Got a liquid diet going?"

He unlocked his truck and dumped the bags on the seat. "You can't fish without beer. It's a rule."

"So that's why my daddy's never caught anything! He always takes orange juice."

"There's exceptions for preachers. Maybe he's just a bad fisherman." Jake closed the car door then looked at her more closely. "You talk to him about your show? You seemed pretty worried last night about what he'd think."

"I spoke with my mom." Sally shook her head. "To say the conversation was bizarre would not do it justice."

"They're mad?"

"No—just the opposite...."

She found herself about to explain more, then broke off abruptly. "God, I didn't come here to bore you with all this...."

"You're not boring me. I asked, remember?"

She looked up into his eyes. She hadn't imagined it. They *were* warmer now, the light blue had darkened into a deep sapphire. She nodded slowly. "I—I guess I just don't understand it."

"And that bothers you. You're the kind of woman who likes to analyze it all, understand why people do what they do."

She looked at him in amazement. "How did you know that?"

He smiled. She hadn't noticed until now how full and perfect his lips were. "I'm not a mind reader—it's just obvious. You've clearly given it a lot of thought already." He shrugged, his wide shoulders moving easily beneath the black T-shirt stretching across his chest. "Why? would be my question. Just accept it. They're happy, you're happy—I'm sure your show will do great. Just go for it and don't worry about why."

"Is that what you do?" she asked.

"Generally speaking, yeah. Doesn't pay to do much else. Can't change fate, right?"

She nodded slowly. Maybe he was right. Maybe she examined things *too* closely sometimes. If her parents had accepted the show, and Rita obviously wanted her to do it, then Sally should be thrilled. It could be her ticket out of Comfort—just as Rita had said. So why wasn't she jumping up and down?

They stood together in the hot sunlight, then slowly, Sally realized Jake was staring at her. She blinked and came out of her thoughts. "I only stopped to say thank you," she said. "You left this morning before I had a chance. I appreciate you coming over before Bob got there."

He put a thumb to the cap perched on his head. *Big Johnson* was stitched across the top. "No problem. It was the quickest thing to do."

"You were a cop in Houston...with Bob?"

"That's right. Twenty years on the force."

"Now what?"

"Now I'm retired." He nodded toward his groceries. "Fishing and drinking. That's my job now."

Sally spoke without thinking. "Retired! You're too young to retire."

He grinned again. "Thanks for the compliment. Unfortunately, you're wrong. I'm almost forty, and that's ancient if you're a cop. Especially a cop with a bum leg."

Her eyes dropped without thinking. "A bum leg?"

His hand went to his upper thigh. "Long story. It seemed like a good time to leave. While I still could."

She started to ask what had happened, then stopped. It was none of her business, was it? And besides, why did she even care? She wasn't looking for a relationship here—she'd only stopped to thank the man, not start up a lifelong commitment.

"You have any more problems, feel free to call, though. I may be retired, but I can still shoot straight."

She smiled. "I'll do that. Hopefully, we won't need the shooting part. I think they just wanted to scare me, that's all."

"You never can tell. Keep my number close."

A few minutes later, he drove away. Sally watched the pickup disappear down the dusty street. She'd been halfway hoping he'd say something about the barbecue Linda had mentioned, but he hadn't. Under a little cloud of disappointment, she turned and headed for the grocery store.

IN HIS REARVIEW MIRROR, Jake watched Sally's figure grow smaller and smaller. There was something about her… She was itching to get away from her life as she knew it, but underneath, he suspected, she was not really as sure as she appeared. The whiskey-rough voice and confident attitude were one thing, but there was a vulnerability behind those soft brown eyes that you didn't notice unless you took the time.

Shaking his head, he aimed the pickup out of town and told himself he didn't *have* the time. Didn't *want* to have the time. A woman like Sally

Beaumont was the last kind of complication he needed. He was on the downswing, ready to kick back and let life roll past him. She was just the opposite—anxious to get out there and see what life was all about. Besides, her new show probably *would* launch her and she'd be outta Comfort like a rocket. She couldn't start a long-term relationship with anyone, much less him.

For some reason, the image of her shattered living-room window came into his mind, bringing with it an uncomfortable thought. Sally was ready to move on for sure, but whoever had thrown that rock might not let her.

4

BY THE TIME Sally got home that evening, Bubba had come and gone. The picture window was as perfect as it had been before, the view of the lake it framed just as soothing and relaxing. Sally tugged off her suit and her panty hose and slipped on a pair of shorts and a T-shirt. Clutching a handful of catfish feed, she padded barefoot down to the water as she did every evening. The dock was long, but by the time she reached the end the water was already roiling with silver flashes and long whiskers that were bobbing up and down with greedy enthusiasm. She flung the food into the water then sat down to watch. The pellets floated for only a few seconds then disappeared, gobbled up by the eager fish.

After seeing Jake, she'd stopped by the church on her way home and talked to her father. He hadn't had much time, but he'd sat down with her, his attitude as caring and gentle as it always was.

"You *aren't* angry?" she'd asked.

"No, honey. Your mother and I have always been proud of you—you know that."

"Except for that time with your new Buick…"

He smiled. "Well, there *was* that time," he acknowledged.

"I thought the show would embarrass you."

His brown eyes crinkled. "Embarrass me?"

"You know…at the church."

He shook his head. "It could get tricky, but if anyone says anything, I'll just point out the need for sex education. Did you know we had four girls at Comfort High get pregnant last year? Four girls! When you were in high school, there was only one…in four years. Our young people need to know more about sex and if your radio talk show can do that, then I say more power to you."

Sally felt a sweep of guilt come over her. He was making her sound like some kind of crusading angel. "Dad…you know the show isn't *exactly* educational.…"

In the light streaming through his office window, she thought she saw a twinkle in his eyes, but once again, Sally didn't trust herself to know that for sure.

"People are calling you and asking questions, right?"

"Well, yes…but—"

"And they need this information? It's not readily available anywhere else?"

"Well, maybe…but—"

"Then it's educational, Sally. It's educational and a public service. If Elmer Holley doesn't know how to find glow-in-the-dark condoms by himself, believe me, you're helping society by leading him in the right direction."

Sally couldn't help herself. She started to giggle, then her father joined her and soon they were laughing out loud—*too* loud for where they were, in a preacher's study.

When they quieted back down, she wiped the tears from her eyes and stared at her dad. "I thought—"

"I know what you thought, honey, but you thought wrong. Your mother and I are grown adults." His eyes did twinkle now. "And we've known about sex for quite a long time."

"That's not what I meant… Your job, your position…"

He dropped his gaze and put his hands on the top of his desk. For a minute, they both stared at those hands, pale and flecked with brown spots. When he spoke, his voice held regret. "This town is full of mighty good people, Sally Anne, but I've got to tell you, it's not the Comfort I knew when I was younger. The narrow-mindedness I've been seeing lately is beginning to bother me.''

For the second time that day, Sally felt her mouth drop open. She'd never heard her father criticize anything or anyone in Comfort. They hadn't had a talk like this in quite a while, either, she realized a moment later.

The door burst open a second after that, a tiny redheaded boy standing on the threshold. ''It's Story Time!'' he yelled. ''We want to hear about Moses and the Ten Combatants.''

Her father stood, then shot a glance toward her and shrugged. ''A new version, I guess.''

Sally grinned at the recollection. Looking into the lake water, she thought about her meeting tomorrow with Rita. She'd say yes to doing the show, she knew. There was nothing standing in her way now...unless you counted the rock.

And, of course, Sally didn't.

SALLY WAS ALMOST READY for bed when the phone rang. It startled her, scared her actually, and she found her heart racing. Maybe the rock had upset her more than she wanted to admit.

Debbie MacAroy's friendly voice answered Sally's tentative hello. ''Sally! This is Debbie! How ya doing?''

Debbie ran the local beauty shop and everything

she said seemed to end with an exclamation point. When she'd first come to Comfort with Bob, after years in Houston, she'd had to relearn how to do hair. In central Texas, your hair wasn't fixed until it stood out from your head at least six inches and was lacquered to a high polish so it could withstand the wind. To Debbie's credit, she'd learned fast. Lots of teasing, lots of spray…and plenty of gossip.

"I'm just fine, Debbie." Sally tried to make her voice sound casual, but her heart hadn't slowed a bit. In fact, it had speeded up. Had Debbie called about the barbecue? Childishly, behind her back, Sally crossed her fingers. "How you doing?"

"We're great! In fact, we're having a party! To introduce a new friend of Bob's around. Well, heck, it's Jake—I'm forgettin' you met him the other night. It's a surprise! He doesn't know a thing about it, but we're all showing up at the cabin on Saturday at noon! Won't that be a hoot! Bring some potato salad and a cooler of soda! Okay? See ya then!"

Sally hung up the phone slowly, a grin spreading over her face. That explained everything, she thought. He hadn't even known about the party….

"AND FIVE … four … three … two … you're on!" Linda pointed to Sally, isolated in the broadcast booth.

Sally's mouth was so dry she couldn't have spit

if her life depended on it, but somehow she managed to get the words out.

"Good afternoon, Comfort. This is Sally Beaumont with *Too Hot for Comfort,* and we're here for your questions. The lines are ready so we'll take callers as they come."

After her meeting with Rita, who'd been thrilled but not surprised by Sally's capitulation, they'd agreed to try and corral the questions by targeting certain topics each day. The station manager had actually liked Rebecca Beaumont's take on the show, too. That it was educational. "Maybe that'll keep out some of the bigger nut cases..." Rita had said.

"Today's subject is sex and alternative lifestyles." Sally took a deep breath. "Any thoughts out there on that?"

While Sally was still speaking, Linda held up her forefinger. A signal to pick up line one. Already! She flashed her other fingers three times. There were calls waiting, too! Sally suddenly wanted to crawl under the desk, but she punched the first button on the phone and answered. "Hi, caller. What's on your mind?"

"What's with this topic business?" It was a man speaking and he sounded cranky. "I got a question and it ain't about alternative life whatevers."

"Okay, then." Sally's heart thudded. "What is your question?"

"I wanna know how many times a week is normal?"

"How many times what is normal?"

"What the hell do you think? This ain't a show about plowing, is it? How many times a week should two people have sex?"

"I—I don't think there's an absolute rule on that, sir. Whatever feels comfortable to both partners is normal."

"Well, gol-darned, what kinda answer is that? How many times a week do *you* do it?"

Outside, in the engineer's booth, Linda doubled over with laughter. She was holding up her hand, making a circle out of her thumb and forefinger.

Sally held up a finger of her own—Linda was *supposed* to be screening calls—then returned to business. "I believe the national average is six times a month, sir. I think that works out to about one-and-a-half times a week."

"How in the hell do you have half-sex?"

"It's just a figure," Sally said hopelessly. "An average number!"

"All right, then. Thass good enough, I guess!" He slammed the phone down so hard Sally's ear rang.

She looked out into the booth. Still all she could

see of Linda was her hand. She held up two fingers, and Sally punched the second phone line.

"Hi, caller. You're on *Too Hot for Comfort*. What's your question?"

"Am I on?"

"You're on."

"Well…I…I like to be on top and my husband likes to be there, too. We're gettin' into some awful fights about who gets to be on top. Have you got any suggestions?"

What the hell had happened to alternative life-styles? Sally wondered if her mother was listening. Was *this* as educational as she'd thought it would be?

"Why don't you try some different positions?" Sally offered. "Something where you're both on top."

"Both…on top? Wh—what do you mean?"

"Lie facing each other. That way neither of you loses. How's that?"

"Ohhh, that sounds kinda interestin'."

"Well, good, I'm glad I helped. And this may help even more… Now we're going to hear from our latest sponsor, Lucy's Secrets. If your love life is flagging, Lucy's got a secret for you. Come on out to Highway 69, and she'll help you select the lingerie that'll do the trick…." Sally pointed to Linda who'd finally managed to get back in her chair. She cued the music and Sally relaxed back in her own seat.

She had only a moment's rest, though, before the next round of questions began. And they didn't end. When the show's hour was up, the phone lines were still flashing. Sally randomly selected one final call, her mind twirling, her brain exhausted.

"Hi, caller. You're on the air. What's your question?"

The voice was tentative and shy. Young, probably a teenager, she imagined, but she couldn't tell if it was a boy or a girl. "It's about your topic," the caller said. "You know, alternative life-styles."

"Yes, go on."

"Well, I'm just wondering how…well, how you know if you want one or not."

"Some people don't think it's a matter of wanting one. Gender identity—which is basically what we're talking about—is something you're born with, they think. You know—like blue eyes or black hair. A strong chin or wide shoulders." As soon as the words were out, she thought of Jake. She shook her head and continued. "Some people believe you're naturally attracted to one sex or the other and that's just how it is. You meet someone, you fall in love with them—it doesn't matter which sex they are."

"Can you change it? That attraction, I mean?"

"Some believe you can," she said carefully. "Some people don't. Are you having some questions about your own identity?"

"No! Nuh-uh. Absolutely not. I—I know what I like. It—it's a friend of mine, you know. I'm asking for him—um—her."

Sally's heart swelled in sympathy. The poor kid was obviously confused and trying desperately to deny it. "I understand. The important thing to tell your friend is that sometimes it takes a while to sort things like this out. Your friend might be confused now, but that's only because when we're young everything's confusing. As we grow older, we sort things out."

"Yeah, right." The caller sounded relieved. "Wow, thanks, man. That really makes sense, too. I mean, what's the rush, right? Got the rest of my life—uh, his life—I mean her life…to decide. Thanks."

Linda cued up the show's canned ending and with a weary sigh, Sally stood, rolling her shoulders. A second later, Rita opened the door. "Damn good show, Sally."

Sally arched her back. "You think?"

"I know!" Rita was usually faint with her praise and Sally couldn't believe her ears. She held up her thumb. "Damn good."

SATURDAY MORNING dawned hot and hotter. Jake slipped on a pair of shorts and his cap and headed for the lake. It was time to do some serious fishing.

With a full cooler and a brimming bait bucket, he climbed into Bob's rattletrap flat-bottomed boat and navigated to the center of the lake. Five minutes later, he had his rod and reel in one hand and a cold Corona in the other. He sat back against the seat in the boat and gave a contented sigh. It just didn't get much better than this.

As soon as he closed his eyes, of course, Sally Beaumont invaded his mind. Leaning up against his pickup truck, those soft brown eyes looking into his. He shook his head. God, she was a good-looking woman. And that voice! Yesterday afternoon, he'd listened to the show—along with everyone else in Comfort, he was sure—and once again, her gravelly voice had made him think of things he shouldn't. Like her underwear. Would it match her voice or her appearance? Prim and proper or lacy and see-through? K-Mart or Lucy's out on Highway 69?

He let the fantasy build, and two hours later—with one helluva dream rattling around in his head—he woke up. Sweaty, sunburned and horny beyond belief, there was only one way to handle it—well, two actually—but one that was acceptable right now. He stood up, peeled off his shorts and jumped into the lake. The water was shockingly cold and it took away his breath—and all evidence of his thoughts of Sally. He swam in circles around the boat for fifteen minutes, then he climbed back in and headed toward the cabin, the little engine behind the boat put-putting with all the force of a sewing machine. A few minutes later, reaching the dock, he jumped from the boat, grabbed his clothes and his tackle box and started up the slope toward the house.

By the time he heard the voices, it was too late. He couldn't do a thing.

Debbie MacAroy was the first one to see him.

"Hey, Jake! Wow! You been fishing or what?" As if in afterthought, she spoke again, explaining why there were fifty strangers behind her, all staring at him in surprise. "Hey! We're having a party for you! To introduce you to everybody! Guess they're going to get to know you real good, huh?" She burst out laughing.

Jake smiled weakly and wished he had more in his hand than a ragged pair of shorts and a plastic box. Thank God he'd bought an extra large one.

"Hey there, Debbie," he said with as much dignity as he could muster. "I wasn't expecting a party or I wouldn't have dressed this casually."

Bob ambled over and joined Debbie. He had two beers in his hands. He held one out to Jake, a mock expression of apology on his face. "I brought this to you, but seeing as how you got your hands full, maybe it ought to wait, huh?"

Jake gritted his teeth. "Think you could help me out here, pal? Get me a towel or something?"

Ignoring Jake's question, Bob glanced down, then back up. "You always fish in the buff? What 'bout them 'skeeters? Don't they getcha?"

"It was hot. I went swimming. I thought I'd just come back up here, shower and then dress. Like I said…I wasn't expecting a party."

From the corner of Jake's eye, he caught a movement and when he saw who it was, he groaned. Sally Beaumont. Great. Just great. She had on white shorts and a tight sleeveless T-shirt, with a long-sleeved shirt tied around her waist. Her legs seemed to go on forever. She was trying hard not to grin but as she reached Bob and Debbie's side, she couldn't hold it back a minute longer. She started to giggle, her eyes crinkling in the corners, her laughter as sexy and deep as her voice. "Hello, Jake! We're having a barbecue at your place today. Guess Debbie forgot to tell you, huh?"

Seeing her grin and hearing that sexy laugh, Jake suddenly couldn't do anything but smile himself. "Hell, no, I knew about it. This is how we dress for barbecues in Houston. Didn't you know?"

Her eyes met his. They were gleaming, still, but

the expression had shifted minutely. ''Can't say as I knew that,'' she drawled. ''Sounds kinda interesting, though. What happens if you drop sauce somewhere you shouldn't?''

''Well, that depends...''

Her eyes were definitely gleaming now. He was sure of it. ''On what?''

''On where it lands and how good a friend you are with the one sitting next to you.''

Before Sally could answer, Debbie leaned over and handed Jake a bath towel. He hadn't even realized she'd left as he'd been talking to Sally. ''Here ya are, Jake! Cover yourself up and go on inside and change! We'll set up the tables and get things going out here.''

His eyes never leaving Sally's, Jake took the towel and draped it around his waist. It was hard going with the tackle box in his hands as well, but he couldn't very well drop one for the other. She kept her gaze on his until he got the towel around him, then she lowered her stare to the blue-and-white striped cotton. Lazily, she brought her eyes back to his face and grinned, then she turned around and walked away.

''OH. MY. GOD. Did you see that butt?'' Linda held a can of beer and a rib, her eyes huge. ''Did you see it, Sally? The man is perfect. I mean perfect.''

Sally sipped her own beer. "Yes. I saw it and yes, it's perfect." Her voice was glum.

Linda looked at her with a puzzled expression. "What *is* your problem? He was eyeing you like you were the last piece of apple pie, and if I'm not mistaken those weren't just casual looks you were sending him, either."

"He's *retired*, Linda! He's in Comfort to fish and drink beer. I don't want a man like that! I'm leaving here as soon as I can, remember?"

"Oh, yeah, right! I forgot there for a minute. You hate your home town and everything in it. That's why you've lived here for six years and haven't left…"

The words hit hard. Sally gave her friend a sharp look. "If you've got something to say, let's hear it. Don't be shy."

Linda took a bite of her rib. "All right," she said, speaking around a mouthful of barbecue. "How's this for honesty? I think you're using your parents as an excuse to stay here. I think you actually do love Comfort and all the nuts that live here and if you did leave, you'd probably be back within a week." She waved the rib in Sally's face. "*That's* what I really think."

"Well, you think wrong," Sally shot back. "Besides, who died and made you the expert psychologist around here?"

Linda grinned. "The same one who died and made you the sex expert!"

Feigning outrage, Sally flounced away and headed toward the buffet. Deep inside she was afraid Linda might be right. In fact, she'd been wondering about this herself, but today Sally wasn't going to think about it. Today, she just wanted barbecue and beer and nothing more stressful than looking at Jake. Who did have the perfect butt and the perfect everything else as far as she could see—which hadn't been far enough. Damn, that tackle box had been big!

Just as she reached the table, the man in question reached her side. He held an empty plate and was about to fill it up. He grinned and held out his hands. "Does this look better?"

No. He now had on blue-jean cutoffs and a black T-shirt, the muscular chest covered, the buff biceps hidden. "Let's just say it's more appropriate," she answered. "How's that?"

He nodded. "Grab a plate, then I want you to tell me about these people hanging around on my lawn."

Sally did as he ordered and together they took heaping platters to a small table someone had set up under the pin oak tree. Jake sat closer to her than she would have sat to him, but she didn't mind. The hard feel of his thigh next to hers was definitely not unpleasant, and sometime between being naked and getting clothed, he'd added a light aftershave, too. Something that smelled really clean and soapy.

"Okay," he said as they settled in. "Tell me who these folks are."

She nodded her head toward the edge of the house. "Well, that's my mom and dad right over there. Did you meet them?"

"No, thank God. I think they came late. Didn't get to see my emergence from the lake."

Sally smiled. "The two women with them are Loretta Smith and Pearl Westbrook. They work at the station. I'm sure they're bending Daddy's ear about how sinful my program is. They couldn't wait until tomorrow after church."

Jake nodded. "And how about them?" He pointed toward another group with his beer can. "They look interesting. That woman in the middle is mighty overdressed. And how does she get her hair to stand up like that?"

It hadn't been necessary for him to point. Sally knew exactly who he meant. "That's Mary Margaret Henley. She's Bob's aunt, twice-removed, and she's currently unhappy with me, too. She was the cooking expert I hired to do the show and when the first question came in, you would have thought I'd stabbed her with a meat carver. She was not pleased.''

''You had no control over the callers....''

''Explain that to her, please.'' Sally shook her head. ''She had plans to be the Martha Stewart of the air waves, but obviously that didn't work out. She left in a huff and hasn't spoken to me since.''

Sally pointed discreetly to Rita March and Linda. They were standing by the dessert table, nibbling cookies with Ricky Carter. Obnoxious and pushy, the man had clearly barged in—they would never have invited him to join them. ''And that's my boss and my best friend. Rita and Linda, with Ricky Carter. He's a recent hire at the station.'' She laughed. ''Linda thinks Rita paid someone to throw the rock through my window so I'd get my back up and stay and do the program. She's a nut.'' Still chuckling, she sent a glance at Jake's profile. He was studying Rita as she pointed them out, she realized all at once, and it wasn't just a casual interest. ''Linda didn't mean it,'' she said suddenly. ''It was a joke. Rita wouldn't do something like that.''

He turned, his laser eyes drilling hers. ''Are you sure?''

Was she sure? All at once, Sally sobered and considered the question. Rita *would* do whatever it took to make the station successful. She was tough and playing in what was basically a man's field.

Still… "I don't think she'd do something to hurt me."

"The rock didn't hurt you. You were sleeping. Anyone looking into the window could see you weren't around."

Pulling in her bottom lip, Sally shook her head slowly. "It's not Rita's style. She's more straight-forward. She told me exactly what she thought about doing the program right up front. She doesn't hold back."

"What about your friend, Linda? Any reason for her to do it?"

"Oh, God, no. Linda's even more up-front." Sally shook her head. "No. No way."

"Then who?" Wiping his mouth on a red, white and blue paper napkin, Jake leaned back and looked at her.

"How about Pearl and Loretta? They're sure I'm meant for hell."

Jake stared at the two women. "Either one of them own a boat?"

"Pearl's husband is a big fisherman. He's got a twin-engine Stinger that'll cross the lake in five minutes. I think I would have heard it, though. It's louder than hell."

"But you said you were sleeping."

She shrugged.

"Anyone else? How about the famous Mary Margaret?"

Sally burst out laughing. "Are you kidding? She wouldn't risk getting her shoes dirty just to toss a rock through my window. Although, I guess she could throw it. Look at those arms. They're made for rolling dough, aren't they?"

They both stared at the overdressed, fussy-looking woman and began to laugh. A few minutes after that, Bob and Debbie came and joined them, Bob explaining to Jake who the rest of the people were, Debbie and Sally occasionally joining in.

By the time dusk had begun to fall, most of the guests had left. Bob and Debbie went last, Bob carrying Brittany in his arms, her shirt smeared with barbecue sauce, one of her tennis shoes missing in action.

"You look for that shoe, now, Jake. Those things cost a fortune these days!" Walking to her car, Debbie spoke, her own arms full of plastic containers. "They still halfway fit her, too!"

Jake promised to look for the shoe, then turned to Sally as Bob and Debbie drove away a moment later. "Do you have to leave now? We could have a nightcap...I've got some Amaretto."

In the full moonlight, his stare was almost magnetic. Somewhere out near the lake, a hoot-owl cried. Sally shivered and suddenly she understood what her father meant when he preached on temptation. "I think it'd be best for me to get on home."

Jake reached out and trailed a finger down her cheek, tucking her hair behind her ear. "Why would that be best?" he said. "I don't think a drink would hurt things, would it?"

"No. Probably not. But…"

He waited.

"But I—I've got to get up early in the morning and go into the station. I need to catch up on my regular work. Since I started the show, everything else got dropped.…"

It was such a patent excuse, there was obviously nothing else he could say. For a second she thought he might argue—hoped he might argue?—then he dipped his head in acquiescence. "All right, then. Guess you know best."

They turned and walked toward her car, Sally already regretting her words, but not knowing exactly how to change them. She opened her mouth to try, then stopped abruptly and gasped. Jake instantly tensed.

"What is it?"

She pointed to her car without a word. All four tires were flat.

Flat and slashed to ribbons.

5

"GO INSIDE." Jake's voice was grim. He didn't really think whoever had slashed Sally's tires was still there, but he didn't want to have to worry about her and look around, too. "Right now. Lock the door and stay there till I come in."

She turned and ran soundlessly back to the cabin. When he heard the door slam shut, Jake began to circle the car slowly. The moonlight was almost as bright as day. In the silvery expanse he could see footprints all the way around the automobile, but none stood out from the rest. Boots, tennis shoes, even someone wearing high heels. Anyone from the party could have done the damage—or actually, anyone could have come up the driveway and done it while they were eating. He looked more closely at the car. It was spotless. No handprints on the side, no muddy hints at all. He stood back and shook his head. Malicious mischief or another warning? A fluttering motion caught his eye and he saw a piece of paper tucked under one of the windshield wipers. Using just the edge of his fingers, he plucked the note out and read it, the printed letters easy to see in the bright light pouring over his shoulder.

THIS IS YOUR SECOND WARNING. COMFORT DON'T NEED SMUT!

With the letter in his hand, Jake went inside. Sally was standing in the center of Bob's small living room, in the glow of a single lamp. She was licking her lips and trying not to look nervous. Her hands gave her away, though; they were twisted together, her long fingers knotted. She darted a quick look at the paper he held and reached out for it.

He managed to yank it back at the very last second. "No—we might get some prints off it!"

She looked startled, but nodded. "Wh—what does it say?"

He held it out and she read it. When she finished, she lifted her eyes to his and said simply. "Oh, shit."

"Yeah, that just about sums it up." He shook his head. "What kind of idiot would get this riled up about a damned talk show? I just don't understand it."

"That's Comfort," she said, slowly sinking into a tattered recliner.

"I've got to call Bob. He'll need to hear about this."

Bob answered on the second ring and listened silently as Jake described the situation.

"I'll drop off Debbie and Brittany and come right back—"

"There's no reason to do that. The car's not going anywhere and I already checked it out as well as you would. Just come out in the morning. I can give you the note then. You ever get any prints off the first one?"

"Oh, hell no. That's gonna take weeks. Might speed things up now, since we got a second one."

They talked for a few more minutes, then Jake hung up. When he went back into the living room, Sally looked at him. She seemed more angry than worried. "I can't believe this," she steamed. "What in the hell is this nut trying to accomplish?"

Jake sat down on the sofa, the old springs complaining under his weight. "You're assuming logical thought there, Sally. Whoever's doing this might not think like you or me." She nodded silently, then he spoke again. "Does it scare you?"

For a second, she played with a gold necklace around her neck. "Kinda."

"Want to stay here?"

Her fingers stilled and she met his gaze. "I—I don't think so."

"Why not?"

She paused, then allowed her big brown eyes to

focus on his. Her voice was an unintentional sexy growl. "It might be more dangerous for me here."

"I could sleep on the couch."

"But we both know you wouldn't."

They stared at each other. She was right, and Jake *did* know it. He didn't really give a damn, though. It was inevitable, wasn't it? From the day he'd heard her voice, he'd known what the outcome would be. Known what he *wanted* it to be.

She rose slowly. "Could you just give me a ride home? I think that'd be the smartest thing."

He stood, too, his gaze locking on hers from across the room. "Do you always do the smartest thing?"

Her mouth parted slightly and she took a deep breath. He could see her chest rise and fall beneath the T-shirt. "Not always, but in this case, I think I'd better. Don't you?"

He didn't answer; he couldn't. He turned and got his keys, then walked outside to his truck, her footsteps echoing behind his a second later.

WHEN JAKE PULLED UP to Sally's house a few minutes later, she was still numb. Numb, and scared, and more confused than she'd ever been in her life. Sally Beaumont was not a woman who moved fast—on anything—and she'd been so tempted to say yes and spend the night with Jake, that it shocked her.

He made her want to do reckless things.

He got out of the truck and came over to her side of the vehicle, then opened her door and held out his hand to help her. She took his warm fingers in hers and slid from the cab, but he didn't move away. Instead, he looked down at her and took a step closer.

Most of his face was in the shadow thrown off by the huge pecan tree that took up half her front yard. She couldn't see his expression, but she could feel the tension in his body. It radiated toward her and enveloped her like some kind of electrical field. She felt trapped.

"I should go inside first," he said. "Just to check out your house. Then I'll leave. I promise."

"Okay," she answered. "That's fine."

But neither of them moved.

Ever so slowly, he raised his hands and placed them on either side of her face. His touch was hot. His fingers stayed still for just a second, then he slid his right palm underneath her hair and behind her neck where he cupped the curve of her head. He tilted her back until her eyes were looking straight into his.

She thought for a moment he was going to say something, but then suddenly he seemed to change his mind. His eyes shifted and so did his expression and a moment later, he lowered his head and began to kiss her.

His lips were fuller and more demanding than she'd expected. When his mouth pressed against hers and his tongue slid forward, she realized he wasn't the kind of man who simply kissed a woman; he had expectations. He wanted what he was giving returned—in spades.

She hesitated, and then it seemed impossible to do anything but kiss him back. Her hands went around his waist and he dropped his to her back, and they moved closer, their lips never parting.

A tingle she hadn't felt in a very long time—if ever—started somewhere in the vicinity of Sally's gut and moved upward. A warmth spread with it, the kind of warmth that starts slow but grows quickly. She wanted Jake. Wanted him naked in her bed, her legs wrapped around him, their hands tangled together, their bodies sweaty and gleaming in the moonlight trapped in the sheets.

His hands slid downward. Her shorts were short and she could feel his fingers as they moved lower to brush exposed flesh. She groaned and he responded, pulling her closer to cup the weight of her bottom, his touch even more insistent, his fingers edging inward.

They stayed that way for a moment, Sally almost

dizzy. Finally, she gasped and pulled back, some shred of common sense finally awakening inside her.

"This—this isn't what I—I planned on," she managed.

He looked down at her, his eyes dark and heavy-lidded, his lips full. "You don't have to plan everything."

"Oh yes, I do."

"Why?"

"I—I've always been that way."

"Then maybe it's time for change, Sally." He said her name with a rumble. She felt it all the way down her body, which responded automatically. *Yes!*

"No." She shook her head. "Pl-planning is best. That way there are no surprises."

"There's always going to be surprises, darlin'. That's life." He tightened his arms around her and she thought he was going to kiss her again. But he didn't. He released her and made her wait on the porch while he checked out her house. It was fine, of course, and he left a few minutes later, promising to help with the car the next day. She went to bed, but she didn't go to sleep.

BOB ARRIVED at the cabin early the next morning, earlier than Jake would have liked. He hadn't gotten a lick of sleep; he'd tossed and turned and dreamed of brown eyes all night long. Finally he'd just gotten up, but he wasn't ready for company—not Bob's, anyway.

The screen door squeaked as Bob pushed it open. "You home?"

"Back here. In the bathroom."

Bob's heavy steps rattled the ancient wood floor. He stopped in the door to the bath, his eyes catching Jake's in the cloudy mirror as he scraped the razor over his cheeks.

"I saw the car," he said. "Helluva mess, huh?"

Jake nodded. "Somebody's mad. They could have just let the air out of the tires and accomplished the same goal."

Bob leaned against the doorway. "Any ideas?"

Jake told him about the three women he and Sally had discussed; Pearl, Loretta and Mary Margaret. Bob shook his head and laughed. "All the usual suspects, right?"

Jake grinned in response. "You got any better ones?"

Bob sobered. "As a matter of fact, I might. I stopped at the station this morning and did something I should have done when the rock went through her window. I called a buddy of mine in DPS and had him run all the names of everyone at

KHRD through their computer. It keeps track of all charges filed, whether they go to trial or not.''

Jake's hand froze, the razor poised between the sink and his face. ''And?''

''There's a new guy down at the station—an electrical engineer by the name of Ricky Carter—''

''He was here yesterday. At the party.''

Bob nodded. ''Yeah, well, he had a party of his own last year in San Antone. Seems he was arrested and charged with assault. He got unhappy with his girlfriend and took a baseball bat to her lawn ornaments.''

Jake turned around slowly and stared at Bob. ''Let me get this straight.'' He paused. ''You found a guy that beat up a ceramic gnome?''

Bob nodded seriously, then arched one eyebrow. ''*Seven* gnomes. And Snow White, too. There were crime scene photos.'' He closed his eyes and seemed to shudder. ''It wasn't pretty, Nolte, I'm here to tell ya.''

''And the reason you think this gnome killer could be behind Sally's problem is…?''

''The guy took the bat to his girlfriend's car after that…and then he tried to get her. He told the arresting office he'd overheard her talking about sex with some of her buddies and he didn't want her talking like that.''

Jake dropped the towel he'd been using to wipe his face. "And Rita March still hired him?"

"She didn't know about it. The girlfriend dropped the charges and he didn't put them on his employment application. I called Rita this morning. She went to the office and checked."

"Sounds promising."

"Yeah." Jake paused. "And there's more... Seems like Mr. Carter asked Sally out when he first moved here three months ago. She turned him down and he was not happy about it. Wrote her some E-mail, telling her what a great thing she was passing up. Sally showed it to Rita, but they both decided to blow it off at the time."

"You think he could be behind the rock and the tires?"

"He might be using the situation just to harass her. Stranger things have happened."

They moved into the kitchen. Jake poured two cups of coffee from the pot he'd brewed earlier. "You tell Sally all this?"

"Not yet." Bob sipped from the cup and grimaced. "Damn! This tastes like sh—"

Jake spoke casually, ignoring the coffee critique. "I'm going over there this afternoon. I'll tell her for you. That way you can go on home..."

Bob met Jake's eyes across the scarred kitchen

counter. "*You're* going to see Sally this afternoon? Why?"

"I offered to help with the car. You know, see to the tires, all that."

Bob's gaze was speculative. "Elmer down at the Exxon usually handles that sort of thing pretty well."

Jake shrugged. "I offered and she accepted. Maybe she didn't want someone who uses glow-in-the-dark condoms messing with her car."

"How does she know *you* don't use 'em?"

Jake lifted his coffee mug and smiled over the rim. "How do you know she doesn't?"

SALLY KNEW HER MOTHER would call when she didn't show up at church that morning so she saved Rebecca the trouble. She phoned her first and gave her a rundown on what had happened to the car and the window.

Her mother was shocked. "Oh, dear. This is terrible. Maybe you should move in with us for awhile. It's not safe out there all by yourself at the lake."

Her answer was exactly what Sally expected, and somehow it made her feel better even as it exasperated her. "Mother, I'm fine. And besides, Jake can get here in five minutes." As soon as she spoke his name, Sally bit her tongue. What was she thinking? If her greatest goal was getting out of town, her mother's was getting Sally married.

"Jake? You mean, Bob's friend. That nice young man at the barbecue yesterday."

Sally closed her eyes. "That's him."

"Well..." Pause. "Are you...seeing him?"

Sally thought of Jake's emergence from the lake. She held back a giggle and dodged the question. "He's...um...helping Bob—with the case."

It took Sally another ten minutes to convince her mother she was fine, then they hung up. And Sally stared aimlessly at the wall over the couch. On a normal weekend after church, she'd drive down to the station, but without a car, she couldn't go into the office and without going into the office, she didn't know what to do. All at once, she realized how much she depended on her work to keep her busy. She had nothing else.

She wandered out to the porch and sat down on the swing. It faced the lake, and as she touched the floor with her toe to set the chair in motion, she let her mind return to the two topics it couldn't seem to leave alone: Who could be doing these bad things to her, and how attracted she was finding herself to Jake Nolte.

Strangely enough, she really wasn't too concerned about the rock or the car. No one in Comfort would want to seriously harm her; they were just trying to let her know they weren't happy. She had thought briefly of canceling the show, but she knew she wouldn't. *Too Hot For Comfort* had the potential to be a hit, and she enjoyed doing it.

No, the main thing on her mind was Jake. Every time she got around him, she felt itchy and hot—as if she were wearing a wool sweater that was too tight. He made it hard for her to breathe and even harder for her to concentrate...on anything but him.

By midafternoon, Sally was about to go nuts. She talked to Linda six times on the phone, she ate almost a whole jar of peanut butter, and she flipped through all the channels on the television set too many times to count. She was bound and determined not to call Jake, though. When the car was ready, he'd show up.

An hour later, he did.

Sally stood in the shade of her front porch and watched him pull into her driveway. He killed the engine of his pickup and climbed out, the hot afternoon sun highlighting his coal-black hair and making it gleam. He had on gold-rimmed sunglasses, jeans and a T-shirt. He walked slowly up to her porch, stopping just short of the steps.

"Your car's ready," he said. "I drove over to Kerrville to the discount place and got you four new tires. Elmer put them on for you. The car's at his shop now so I'll take you on over and you can pick it up.''

Sally had never thought of tires as a topic for romance, but the fact that he'd driven all that way just to save her some money... ''You didn't have to do that,'' she said. ''But I sure do appreciate it.''

''I didn't mind. I figured you'd pay me back... one way or another.''

Did everything the man say have sexual overtones...or was it just her? ''I—I will pay you back. My purse is inside. I'll write you a check.''

He took two more steps to come up on the porch where she was holding the screen door. Taking off his glasses, he looked at her. ''Actually, I was hoping for something more than a check.''

Her heart began to thud inside her chest.

''It's awful hot,'' he said. ''How 'bout a glass of something cold and wet?''

Her legs went weak, and she smiled faintly. ''Sure. I—I think I can manage that.'' She held the door open wider and he brushed past her. Or at least he started to. He stopped halfway through the door and looked down at her. His eyelashes were way too long and dark, she thought suddenly, her mouth going dry at his closeness. A man shouldn't be allowed to have eyelashes like that. It wasn't fair.

''Was your night all right?'' he asked. ''No unwanted visitors?''

Only you in my dreams. "I—it was fine. Went right to sleep and never even woke up once."

His eyes pierced hers. She was lying like a big dog and he knew it. "Good," he said slowly. "I'm glad. Me, too."

Sally swallowed hard. A lump had lodged in her throat and she was having a hard time breathing. Finally, he stepped past her and entered the living room. Even though he'd been inside before, she hadn't quite realized at that time how much he seemed to fill up the space.

He nodded toward the picture window, but his eyes never left hers. "Got your glass repaired."

"Yes."

"Nice view."

"Thanks."

They met an instant later somewhere in the middle of the room. Sally wasn't sure who moved first, but it didn't seem to matter. All she knew was that one moment she was standing there, wishing he'd kiss her, and the next moment he was, his arms wrapped tightly around her, her breasts pushing against his chest. He murmured something deep and low in his throat. She didn't know what it was, and she didn't really care. All she could think about was his mouth on hers...his firm, wide lips, his warm insistent tongue, his hands...his hands that were everywhere at once.

They held on to each other as if to let go would court disaster. Finally, one of them came up for air. Stunned, Sally leaned back in the circle of Jake's arms and looked up at him.

"Wh-what's going on?"

"I think that's called kissing."

She shook her head. "That's not like any kissing I've ever encountered before."

"Then I guess you haven't been kissing the right guy."

Her heart flipped over. Twice. Then she reluctantly stepped back from him, breaking the embrace. "Jake—I—I don't know how to tell you this, but I'm not looking for a relationship right now."

"Good," he said. "Neither am I."

She blinked. "You aren't?"

He shook his head.

"But…" His words left her confused, a little disappointed, maybe even a little angry.

"Every kiss doesn't mean something cosmic, Sally. Sometimes a kiss really is just a kiss. Don't analyze it, okay? Just sit back and enjoy the ride."

"Sometimes a kiss is just a kiss." She repeated the words, as if trying them out.

"That's right." He took up the space she'd put between them, then bent over and brushed the corner of her mouth with his lips. It was just a simple touch, not even sexual, but it sparked something deep inside her, and suddenly she wasn't so sure he wasn't lying.

Sometimes a kiss is just a kiss...

She looked up at him, into those deep blue eyes, her mind spinning like the reels down at the station. *Yeah,* she thought suddenly, *and sometimes it's a helluva lot more.*

6

"I JUST DON'T KNOW how to describe it." Sally looked at Linda helplessly. "I've never felt this way before."

They were sitting at the Dairy Queen eating lunch. Well, Linda was eating. Sally was poking at the taco salad she'd ordered and trying to describe her feelings. They'd already discussed the astonishing news Jake had told her about Ricky Carter and they'd moved on to something more interesting— Jake himself.

"You're really falling for this guy, aren't you?" Linda had wonder in her voice. "Man, after all these years…I can't believe it."

"I am not *falling* for anyone! I just…I just find him very appealing, that's all. And it's purely physical." The last came as an afterthought, then Sally realized it was true. She didn't really know anything about Jake beyond the barest of backgrounds. "I don't even know the guy."

"What's it worth to you to know more?" Linda speared a cherry tomato from Sally's bowl and waved the fork over the table in a grandiose gesture. "I might be able to help you out."

"What do you mean?"

She popped the whole tomato into her mouth and spoke around it. "Debbie told me all about him. I got the goods."

Sally wanted to act disinterested, but there was no way she could. Not after Sunday afternoon. Not after *that* kiss. She leaned across the table. "Give it up."

"Well, he grew up in Houston and lived there all his life. He's divorced. Was married five years. Her name was Sandra and she was a witch with a 'b.' Hated the fact he was a cop and gave him a hard time about everything. They went their separate ways and she hooked up with a computer salesman from Spokane."

Sally waved her hand. "Go on, go on..."

"Obviously they had no kids, but according to Debbie, he loves children. He's Brittany's godfather and always gives her incredible presents for her birthday and at Christmas. When he and Bob were partners back in Houston, he used to do volunteer work on his days off at a downtown shelter for homeless kids."

"Why'd he leave Houston?"

Linda squeezed more dressing out of a plastic container onto her salad, then answered. "He was shot during a robbery and after he recovered, he decided he'd had enough. He retired and moved here.''

Shot! Sally was stunned. My God, no wonder he wanted nothing more than peace and quiet. Who wouldn't?

''HI, CALLER, you're on the air. What's your question?''

''It's my boyfriend. He's…um…pressuring me, ya know? To…you know…do the nasty. I don't…you know…know what to do 'cause I ain't too interested in becoming a mama.''

Sally moved closer to the mike. Finally a question she could handle. The morning's show had been a tough one, the topic—methods of birth control—ignored as always. She'd answered questions on everything from her mother's favorite—bondage—to Viagra, and quite a few points in between. She and Linda had started handing out imaginary ribbons to the ''Winner of the Day.'' Qualifications for getting the award varied, but it had begun to boil down to the weirdest caller. Today's choice would be an easy one. It'd have to be the one guy with the heifer… Oh, yeah. There was definitely some serious sexual dysfunction going on there.

''How old are you, caller?''

MILLS & BOON®

An Important Message from The Editors of Mills & Boon®

Dear Reader,

Because you've chosen to read one of our romance novels, we'd like to say "thank you"!

And, as a **special way** to thank you, we've selected <u>two more</u> of the <u>books</u> you love so much **and** a welcome gift to send you absolutely <u>FREE!</u>

Please enjoy them with our compliments...

Tessa Shapcott

Editor, Mills & Boon

P.S. And because we value our customers we've attached something extra inside...

EDITOR'S "THANK YOU" SEAL

PEEL OFF AND PLACE INSIDE

How to validate your Editor's Free Gift "Thank You"

1. **Peel off the Free Gift Seal** from the front cover. Place it in the space provided to the right. This automatically entitles you to receive two free books and a beautiful gold-plated Austrian crystal necklace.

2. **Complete your details** on the card, detach along the dotted line, and post it back to us. No stamp needed. We'll then send you two free novels from the Modern Romance™ series. These books have a retail value of £2.55, but are yours to keep absolutely free.

3. **Enjoy the read.** We hope that after receiving your free books you'll want to remain a subscriber. But the choice is yours - to continue or cancel, any time at all! So why not accept our no risk invitation? You'll be glad you did.

Your satisfaction is guaranteed

You're under no obligation to buy anything. We charge you nothing for your introductory parcel. And you don't have to make any minimum number of purchases – not even one! Thousands of readers have already discovered that the Reader Service™ is the most convenient way of enjoying the latest new romance novels before they are available in the shops. Of course, postage and packing to your home is completely FREE.

Tessa Shapcott
Editor, Mills & Boon

"I'm thirteen and I—I don't live 'round Comfort. I'm from…um somewhere else."

"Well, you're smart to be thinking about the consequences of having sex so young. Being a parent is a scary thing, especially for someone who isn't ready."

"Yeah, yeah, I know. But…" The voice grew tentative and then died out.

Sally wanted to reach through the mike and give the poor girl a hug. "You probably think you're going to lose him, right?"

"He told me if I didn't give him what he wanted, there were plenty of girls who would, you know? And I don't wanna lose my boyfriend. I…I don't got nobody else."

"Do you have a mom and dad at home?"

The voice turned sullen. "Yeah, kinda. My mom…and a stepdad."

"Can you talk to them about this?"

"Oh, sure! Right! I can see that happening…."

Sally felt the pressure build behind her eyes. This kid was all alone and facing serious stuff. "What if you relented and gave your boyfriend what he wanted? Is that a guarantee he'd stay?"

Silence came over the line. "I—I don't know. I hadn't thought about it."

"Well, let's think about it now. You could have

sex with him, and that still doesn't mean he'd be there forever, right?''

The answer was slow in coming, but it came. "Yeah. He could bug out anytime.''

"That's right.''

"So...what you're saying is giving in to him don't mean I'll get what I want. It just means he'll get what he wants.''

Sally held a long breath then expelled it quietly. "That's exactly right. He'd get everything—and you might end up with a disease or a baby. The first thing you said was you didn't want to be a mama. Becoming a parent is something everyone having sex should think about long and hard. You're very smart to be considering it now...before it's too late.'' Sally started to click off, then she stopped. "Call me back, okay? Let me know what happens.''

"Yeah...yeah, I might do that. And thanks...''

WHEN SALLY came to the front door of the office later that evening, Jake was leaning against the fender of *her* car, waiting for her just as she had waited for him that day at the grocery store. She paused before stepping outside to watch him for a moment. Though he wore his sunglasses, she could tell his eyes were sweeping the parking lot, from one side to the other, slowly, thoroughly. He appeared to be looking for something or someone other than her.

He had on pressed slacks and a white pullover shirt with short sleeves that showed off his growing tan and taut biceps. His body language was interesting; he was alert, tense, but leaning against her fender as if he didn't have a care in the world. She opened the door and headed for where he stood.

As she approached, he smiled appreciatively. "Hi, there!"

"Hi, yourself." She was suddenly glad she'd worn her best suit to work that day. It was white with blue trim and she had on white pumps that went with it. "What's going on?"

"I was in the neighborhood and realized I was hungry. How about driving over to Medina with me? I hear there's a good steak house there."

She answered without thinking. It was the only way she could; if she thought about it, she would have said no, and she really didn't want to do that. "A steak sounds great."

They walked to his pickup side by side. She glanced up at him. "Did you hear the show?"

"Never miss it."

"What'd you think?"

He opened the car door for her and helped her inside. She sat down, then looked at him expectantly. "I think you gave some damn good advice," he said. "Especially to that last kid—the thirteen-year-old." He shook his head. "She's under some kind of pressure. I really felt sorry for her."

"I did, too." In the evening dusk, they looked at each other and something seemed to pass between them. A shared concern for kids who were alone, for kids who had questions but no answers and no one to turn to for help.

He closed the door and walked around to his side of the truck. A moment later they were pulling away from the station and heading toward the highway.

"When I came out of the station…"

"Yeah?" His voice was noncommittal.

"You seemed to be looking for someone."

"I was." He glanced at her then back at the road. "You."

"No one else?"

He glanced over at her again. They were driving west, into the sun. Behind his glasses she could see nothing but a glare. "I was looking for Ricky Carter," he confessed after a second.

She tensed. "Did Bob hear something else about him?"

Jake shook his head. "No, no. Nothing like that." He let the words die out and silence built inside the cab.

It hit her a second later. "You were hoping he'd

see you…waiting for me.'' Her voice held surprise and amazement.

He shrugged and said nothing.

A ribbon of warmth curled inside her chest. He wanted to protect her, keep her safe. No one had ever done that kind of thing for her before. Of course, she'd never needed it before, either, but it instantly made her feel wonderful.

…sometimes a kiss is just a kiss…

Sure, it was…

JAKE PULLED UP in front of the restaurant, parked, then opened Sally's door. Five minutes later they were sitting in a darkened booth, menus the size of the Houston phone book in their hands. He took one quick glance, then set the tome down. She studied hers for almost two full minutes. He watched her perfect face as she read each selection, considered it, then rejected it. In a way, it was amusing…and in another way it was scary. Had she studied him that carefully, too?

He didn't know why he cared—except that her lips were so damn soft and her curves so damn appealing that when they weren't together, he couldn't get either of them out of his brain. She was smart, too, smart and funny and caring. Before coming to Comfort, he didn't think women like Sally existed anymore. The ones he'd dated after

Sandra had been just like Sandra: hard, selfish and egotistical.

Sally finally put down the menu then looked at him from across the table. There was a small red candle in the center between them and the flame of it danced in the breeze from an overhead fan. Her brown eyes gleamed in the light.

"I found out something about you today," she said slowly.

"And that was?"

"That you worked with kids back in Houston. Homeless kids. Is that true?"

"Yeah, it's true. Debbie been flapping her mouth?"

"Nothing's a secret in Comfort. You ought to know that by now." She put her arms on the table and stared at him. "Why that? Why homeless kids?"

"I saw too many youngsters living on the streets in Houston. I'd take them to the shelters every night, and one thing just led to another. Before I knew it, I was spending my Saturdays down there, too."

"Did you enjoy working with them?"

He thought carefully then answered. "I don't know that 'enjoy' is the right word. I felt like I was able to do some good, and when I was there, I didn't think about my own problems, as pitiful as they were in comparison. In a way it was selfish of me—I did it to help myself as much as the kids.''

The waitress came, took their orders, then left. Sally reached for a piece of bread from the basket the woman had placed in the center of the table.

"That's how it always works," she said, tearing the roll into smaller, dainty pieces. "You never do some good that a little bit doesn't rub off on you. That's to be expected."

"Is that what's happening to you?"

She lifted her eyes. "What do you mean?"

"With the show. Are you getting something good out of that?"

"I had no altruistic motives for that show, believe me. I want out of Comfort and a hit could be the way that happens."

"But you're helping people."

She waved her hand in the air, bread crumbs flying. "I don't know…"

"Well, I know. And so does that teenager who called today." He pursed his lips and made a kissing sound. "And so does that guy who's in love with his heifer. He definitely needed some help and I'm sure the cow's appreciative, too!"

She burst out laughing and shook her head. "You think? Bovine intervention? God, I am a friend to man and animals, alike! Who'da thought it?"

Their drinks came and over the cold draft beer,

Jake spoke slowly. "Tell me about your parents," he said. "When I suggested you stay with them that first day you seemed real reluctant. How come? I thought you had the perfect childhood growing up here."

She took a long swallow of her drink, her throat moving so seductively in the candlelight, he couldn't take his eyes off her. She put the glass down carefully and spoke. "I'm an only child. My parents love me dearly and I love them. But sometimes they smother me. They're very conservative and very careful and I've been the focus of their lives since the day I was born." She played with a napkin on the table. "Because they've always been so involved in my life, I've always felt…I don't know…almost responsible for them, in a way. Like I have to do really well, you know…so they're happy."

"Is that why you came back to Comfort after college?"

"I knew it would please them," she confessed, "but jobs were scarce. When I found this one, I knew I should grab it."

Jake couldn't help himself; he reached across the table and took her hand in his. "You aren't really responsible for them. You know that, don't you?"

"I know. But I love them and I wanted to do the

right thing." She shook her head. "They'll live in Comfort forever. I just hope I don't."

OVER DESSERT, he asked her about her plans. "Why do you want to leave Comfort so much? It doesn't seem all that bad to me."

She leaned back against the booth, her fingers still wrapped around her coffee mug. It'd been a fantastic evening. They'd eaten so much she felt stuffed and they had talked about everything under the sun. At his question, she tensed, though, and she didn't exactly know why.

"I'm tired of living in a place where everyone knows your business. You can't sneeze without someone down the street saying 'God bless you.'"

He raised one dark eyebrow. "There's worse things they can say."

"I know, I know." She leaned closer to him. "Here's a perfect example, though. Mabel Slider and her first cousin are sitting one table over. By sunrise tomorrow, everyone in Comfort will know we were here and that we shared a piece of apple pie for dessert. Doesn't that bug you?"

"Not really. Now if you'd wanted lime pie, yeah, but apple—"

She swung a mock fist in his direction and grazed the brick wall of his shoulder. He caught her fingers with his and held them fast. She could almost feel the burn of Mabel's stare.

Her voice came out breathless. "And now they'll know we were holding hands."

He brought her fingers up to his lips and kissed them one by one. "And what will they say after that…?"

Her breath came fast and in shortened gulps. "That they were sure the hand-holding was followed by a night of wild debauchery. I already have that reputation, you know. After all, I'm the S.E.X. expert."

"It seems a real shame they have to make that up. Can't we at least give them a little something to base it all on?" Without waiting for her to answer, he suddenly leaned across the table and pressed his lips against hers in a gentle but insistent kiss. He tasted of coffee and apple pie and desire. The room dissolved into a haze of nothingness and she melted under the promise of his mouth.

When he pulled back a second later, she was breathing even harder than she had been before. They got up and left, walking past Mabel's table without another glance, their eyes locked on each other, one thing on their minds.

7

SHE WASN'T SURE where Jake was taking them, but after they got in the truck and drove off into the darkness, Sally didn't care. She was sitting close to him in the pickup, and he'd draped his arm over her legs, pulling her even closer. His thigh was pressed against her own, and a tense awareness filled the cab. He wanted to make love to her.

She wanted him, too.

He reached over and turned on the radio. The soft, sexy voice of the nighttime DJ—Dee Loving—wafted out. At six foot four, with a ragged goatee and tattoos up and down his arms, he looked more like a Hell's Angel than a nighttime disc jockey, but his program was one of the most popular at the station. There were a lot of lonely people in Comfort after ten o'clock. They constantly called with requests for forlorn songs and dedicated them to lovers long gone. Sally didn't listen often; it made her sad. She closed her eyes now, though, and let the music wash over her. The sound of the song mingled with the warmth coming from Jake's body and the smell of his aftershave. For just one second, Sally let herself wonder what it might be like if they were having a relationship. A *real* relationship…the kind that led to the altar and children and PTA and all the stuff that went with being a family.

It was a curious sensation. She'd never allowed herself to seriously contemplate that idea with any other man. Why now? Why Jake? Sure, he was handsome and sexy and smart and he could melt her with a kiss, but she had things to do, places to go. She couldn't let him get in the way of that, could she? Without being really conscious of what she was doing, Sally began to examine the situation from every angle she could think of, her analyzing mind picking it apart and putting it back together a thousand different ways.

The next thing she knew, the truck was slowing and had stopped. She looked around and realized they were on the west side of the lake. It was spread out in front of them, and the water shone like a mirror, the reflection of the summer moon a wavery silver disk that seemed to float on top. Jake rolled down both the windows then turned off the engine. The sweet smell of pine immediately came into the cab, along with the kind of sudden silence that only a summer night can hold. Complete and utter quiet. After a bit, the stillness faded and was replaced by crickets and owls and a soft wind dancing through the leaves.

Jake turned to her, his arm along the back of the seat, his fingers curling softly around her shoulder. "I found this spot the other night," he said, leaning closer. "I got lost, made a wrong turn. After I figured out where I was, I wanted you to see it, too."

His breath was warm against her cheek. Sally was sure he could hear her heart, it was pounding so fast and so loudly. "It is beautiful," she said.

"Do you know where we are?" He leaned closer and nuzzled her ear. His lips were soft, but his cheeks were rough. The combination of the two sensations—a feathery touch and a scratchy rasp—was almost more than she could bear.

"N-not exactly."

"Look straight ahead." His voice was a low growl, sexy and deep. "Across the lake."

She didn't want to look at anything; she wanted to turn and face him then rip off all his clothes, but she took a deep breath and did as he instructed. In the distant black, all she could see were two twinkling lights. They looked as if they were side by side, but she knew better. The span between them was distorted by their position across the water.

"It's your house," he said quietly. "Your house and Bob's cabin. You didn't know you could see them from this road?"

She shook her head. "I had no idea."

He eased a finger down her cheek. The touch was soft and barely there, but she felt it. Oh, boy, did she feel it! The warmth of his skin, the barest scrape of his nail, the tiniest hint of what might come. All her senses seemed heightened, on alert.

"You can walk all the way around the lake from here and get to our backyards without a soul seeing you. I went that way the other night," he said. "And I saw you through your window. You really should close your drapes at night."

"I—I don't have drapes."

In the moonlight his eyes gleamed. "Do you understand what I'm saying, Sally? Whoever threw that rock through your window could have easily parked in this spot, hiked around the lake, then tossed the rock and run back here. They didn't have to come down your drive or even approach in a boat."

She nodded and looked back across the water. Her porch light twinkled in the distance then seemed to flicker and go out. It was only the wind, moving limbs and leaves between her house and where she sat, but for a second, her heart stuttered.

Jake took her chin between his thumb and finger and turned her to face him again. "There's someone out there—some kind of nut—who doesn't approve of what you're doing, and it's beginning to make me nervous.''

Sally's pulse hammered, but that was because of Jake's closeness, not his words. ''No one would hurt me here in Comfort,'' she said.

''You don't know that for sure.''

''Jake, please…the most serious crime we've had in the past five years was when Royce Lee's barn was torched. Royce only had his '57 Chevy inside, but that car was his pride and joy. It took Bob a day to figure out Royce had a girlfriend *and* a wife and they'd found out about each other. They wanted to teach him a lesson. One of 'em poured the gasoline and the other lit the match.''

Jake chuckled, but his eyes weren't laughing. ''I hear what you're saying, babe, but this could be more serious. People who get riled up about stuff like this don't always have a good handle on reality and that makes them unpredictable. It could be a rock through the window today but tomorrow it could be a shot from a .22. I don't want that happening to you.'' He paused then tightened his fingers around her shoulder. ''I brought you here so you could see what I was talking about. I want you to get some drapes and I want you to be careful.''

''Anything else?''

He looked thoughtful for a moment, a slight frown marring his forehead before it cleared and his eyes captured hers. "As a matter of fact, yes. There is one more thing…"

"What's that?"

He pulled her toward him and lowered his head, his mouth almost covering hers. "Just this," he murmured. "Just this…"

SHE'D BEEN EXPECTING him to kiss her, but Sally still wasn't prepared. Just as before, his mouth felt soft and demanding, yet this time, there was even more to the kiss. She wouldn't have thought it possible, but he seemed to want an even deeper response from her than he had before. His hands were warmer, his tongue slicker, his murmurs more determined. She responded before she could even think about it.

They kissed for one long moment, then Jake pushed her gently away. Startled, she looked at him, then she realized what he was doing when he moved closer to her and out from under the steering wheel. With his hands on her shoulders he turned her around then pulled her into his lap. The position was even more intimate, and Sally's breath caught in her throat as he began to slowly unbutton her jacket. Through the haze of her growing desire, she wondered about the sanity of what they were doing. Two grown-ups, sitting in a car, making out like teenagers. It seemed preposterous, but it felt absolutely delicious. She wasn't about to stop it from happening.

Instead, she concentrated on the moment. The cool breeze as it came into the truck and caressed her skin. Her exposed bra that shone in the moonlight. Jake's hands as they covered the delicate cups a moment later. He groaned and bent his head to kiss the slope of her breasts, then he dipped lower, his mouth replacing his hands as he gently sucked her nipples through the lace.

She groaned and arched her back, the wet feel of his tongue a teasing torment. Holding the weight of each breast, he brought them closer and buried his face between them. Again she felt the contrast of his warm soft hands and his face, stubbled and rough. In the morning, she'd have reminders of his beard, but now—at this moment—nothing mattered but getting closer to him.

She reached for his shirt and slowly began to unbutton it. When it fell open, she slipped her hands inside and let them slide over his chest. It was hard and firm and she pressed herself against him, even the barrier of her bra too much. As if sensing her thoughts, Jake reached around and undid the clasp. She slipped out of her jacket, then he helped her shed it all before pulling her closer. Skin to skin, they held on to each other in the cab of the truck, Sally's heart thundering, nothing more important to her now than feeling Jake, kissing Jake, wanting Jake.

With one arm wrapped around her, he slid his hand under her skirt and started to kiss her again, his lips so perfectly melded to hers, Sally wondered why she'd ever bothered to kiss anyone else. This was what it was all about, she wondered with part of her brain. This was what they talked about in the movies, what you read about in the books—this was it! She was so deep into the feeling of his hands, his mouth, his touch, it took more than a second to realize something was wrong—terribly wrong—and by then it was too late.

The cab of the truck filled with blinding light and a deep, disembodied voice spoke from out of the darkness. "Excuse me for interrupting folks, but could you please step out of the car and let me see some ID?"

JAKE'S FIRST IMPULSE was to reach under the seat and pull out his .45; then he remembered where he was. This was Comfort, not Houston. The guy with the flashlight wasn't someone out to rob them—he was wearing a uniform and had his own gun on his hip, even though he barely looked old enough to shave.

Holding a hand above his eyes to keep the glare

out, Jake shielded Sally with his chest and spoke to the kid. "How 'bout dousing the light there, son?"

"Please step out of the vehicle, sir."

Bob had trained 'em well.

"Go ahead," Sally whispered at his back. "I— I think I'm decent."

Jake eased open the door and stepped outside. "My wallet's in my pocket," he said. "I'm going to reach inside and get it."

The black metal flashlight beamed a steady path between them. "That's fine."

Jake removed the folded leather wallet slowly, then opened it to his Texas driver's license. He handed it to the young officer.

A second later, the kid gulped; Jake could actually hear him. "Y-You're Jake Nolte? Sheriff Mac's friend?"

"That's me."

"Hot damn, sir, I'm sorry! I—I didn't know. Sheriff told us to keep an eye on this spot and that's what I was doing. I saw your truck with the lights off and everything, and I didn't even think it might be you. Golly, sir, I'm sorry. I—"

"It's okay, son." Jake took his ID back and slipped it into his wallet. "You're doing your job and that's what you're supposed to be doing. I guess you radioed in before you got out of the cruiser?"

"Oh, yessir! That's SOP."

Jake nodded wearily. Great, just great! Bob would never let him live this one down. Never in a thousand years...

The deputy touched his fingers to his cap and started backing up. "Well, you two have a nice night now." He nodded in the direction of Jake's back. "See you later, Sally Anne. Take care."

A faint voice came from behind Jake. "See ya later, Billy Ray. You watch out, too."

Jake stood still until the officer got back into his car and drove away. He then turned slowly and looked at Sally. She was standing barefoot in the pine needles, her hair twisted and mussed. He'd kissed off all her lipstick and she'd buttoned her jacket wrong; it hung lopsided with a teasing gap right in the front that allowed him a tiny glimpse of bare breast.

"Want to start over?"

She shook her head. "I think we'd better get home. I have a clean record—I want to keep it that way."

SALLY WATCHED Jake's taillights disappear down the driveway. He'd walked her to the door, checked out her house, then finally let her go inside. But not before he'd kissed her once...and then once again.

Touching her swollen lips with her fingertips, she

closed the front door and locked it. What was happening to her? What was Jake doing to her?

"Turning my life upside down," she answered out loud in the empty silence of her home. "He's turning it upside down and inside out."

Dangling her pumps in one hand and her purse in the other, she walked into the kitchen where she dropped both things on the countertop and opened the refrigerator door. She reached inside for the milk, opened it and drank straight from the white plastic jug. She had to get a grip on her life. Things at the station were just about to break—she could feel it—and when they did, she didn't want her thinking clouded with images of Jake Nolte and his bright blue eyes.

The light in the refrigerator cast a ghostly shadow against the kitchen's cabinets. She stared at it in the darkness. Her plan didn't include him...or his kisses...or the deep ache she was feeling right now inside her, the ache that had started the minute he'd picked her up outside the station and taken her away.

So what was she going to do?

She replaced the milk carton and shut the refrigerator door. Leaning against it, she closed her eyes and thought. Thought of his fingers against her throat and the feel of his chest under her hand. She thought of the chances she had of ever finding another man who could kiss her like Jake. She thought of her show and where it might take her.

After a moment, she turned and walked through the darkened house to her bedroom. She stripped off her clothes and fell into bed...and wished he was lying beside her.

RITA CALLED SALLY into her office bright and early Monday morning. When Sally passed by her desk, Tiffany's eyes were so narrow and suspicious, she knew immediately word had spread. Mabel had done her duty and told everyone she could that she'd seen Sally and Jake at the restaurant. Actually, Sally had already guessed as much. In church on Sunday morning, she'd gotten a few stares, but she'd thought it was because of the show. She hadn't suspected Mabel was *that* efficient.

Without saying a word, Sally smiled sweetly at Tiffany and went into the inner sanctum.

Rita took off her reading glasses as Sally came in and pointed to one of the chairs in front of her desk. "Have a seat. I just finished a phone conversation I think you'd like to hear about."

Sally went tense. There was only one thing Rita could mean. She'd gotten a call about the show either from an affiliate or another local—but larger—station. Sally sat down, gripped the arms of the chair and looked at her boss. One side of her brain was screaming "Oh, yes!" while the other side was shrieking "Oh, no!"

"KFFD in Austin just phoned. The manager of that station was here last week visiting his aunt, who happens to be Cora Bayliss."

Sally closed her eyes for just a second. Cora was the church secretary, her *father's* secretary. When the church doors were open, Cora was there. Monday through Monday. Rain or shine. Cora was one of the faithful. She always wore the same thing— her trademark floral dress—but on Sundays she added a hat. It offered a nice counterpoint to the sour expression she inevitably wore on her face.

The image of a male version of Cora formed in Sally's mind, and the elation she had first felt at Rita's words leaked out like air from a pricked balloon.

Twirling her glasses between her fingers, Rita leaned back in her chair and stared at Sally. "Cora had the radio on in the kitchen when *Too Hot* came on. She ran across the kitchen so fast to turn off the radio that she tripped over Babycakes and fell down."

Cora's nasty white poodle was as cranky and sour as her mistress. They were a good pair. Sally told herself she was a wicked woman for wanting to laugh, but a giggle escaped before she could stop it. "I—I hope she wasn't hurt."

Rita's expression stayed neutral. "Oh, Babycakes was fine, but Cora sprained her ankle. The nephew took her over to the clinic in Kerrville, then he brought her back here and waited on her hand and foot for the rest of the week. Guess what he listened to every day while Cora was knocked out with her pain pills?"

Sally gasped. *"Too Hot for Comfort?"*

Rita dropped her glasses on her desk and leaned forward, putting her elbows on the edge. "You got it. He thought the show was hysterical, but when he heard you answer that kid—the one whose idiot boyfriend was pressuring her to have sex—that's when he really got interested. He said you had a real feel for dealing with teenagers, and that just happens to be their latest targeted market." She leaned back and steepled her fingers. "He's interested, Sally. Very interested."

Sally's heart thudded inside her chest, hitting her ribs with an almost painful intensity. "Where do we stand right now?"

"He wants tapes of everything—all the shows since the beginning—and he's going to play them for the owner of the station. Howard Atlas is a real hands-on kind of guy and he personally approves— or disapproves—of everything KFFD acquires."

Sally nodded nervously, her stomach churning.

Rita stared at her. "Have you ever heard that name before? Howard Atlas?"

Through the fog of her anxiety, Sally tried to concentrate. "It does sound kinda familiar."

"He owns two stations in Austin…"

"Ohmigod!"

"And one in San Antonio." Rita arched her perfectly plucked eyebrows. "He's got three more scattered across west Texas."

Sally fell against the back of her chair, her hand against her chest. "Are you kidding me?"

Rita ignored her question. "This is important, Sally. For the station and for you. KFFD is very interested and though they haven't made us an offer yet, it could be coming. I know you had some reservations about doing the show at first and I want to make sure you don't have those qualms anymore. If you have any concerns, now is the time to talk about them." Her steely gaze caught Sally's and wouldn't let it go. "*After* we start talking to KFFD is *not* the time. Do you understand what I'm saying?"

"I understand." Sally nodded slowly. Rita couldn't have spelled it out any clearer. Her reputation—and that of KHRD—was on the line, along with Sally's. "I—I do understand…"

"So tell me."

"Tell you what?"

"Tell me you don't have any more qualms. About the show, about the content, about anything.

Tell me the only thing you'll ask is 'how high?' when KFFD says 'jump.'"

"How high?" Sally said tightly. "I got it... How high?"

JAKE HAD TRIED to lay low and stay out of sight, but he'd known it wouldn't last forever. He was in town, washing his truck, when Bob finally caught up with him.

The black-and-white slowed as it passed Jake then it did a U-turn in the middle of the street. Wheeling into the driveway of the three-stall car wash a second later, the cruiser stopped. Through the windshield, Jake could see Bob pick up his mike and call in to Dispatch. A moment after that, he opened the car door and sauntered over to where Jake stood, the pressurized wand in his hand spitting out the last of its soapy water.

"Hey, there, Jake. How's it going?"

Bob pretended to act casual, his hands in his pockets, his face neutral behind his mirrored sunglasses. Jake knew him too well, though.

"Go ahead on," Jake drawled. "You're here to pull my chain, so you might as well start yankin'. The quicker you start, the sooner you'll be finished."

"I swear I don't know what you're talking about, Jake." Bob's expression looked sincere. "You in some kind of trouble or something?"

"You know damn good and well what I'm talking about." Jake turned, the hose still in his hand. Bob did a quick step back to avoid the spray. "Your pup of a deputy is too good. I'm sure you have all the details, including a written report."

"That I do...that I do." Bob leaned against the wall of the car wash. "Including the name of the lady involved. You getting serious with Sally Anne, Jake?"

"Not as serious as I would have if Deputy Dog hadn't intervened."

"You'll have other opportunities...if she wants you to."

Jake flipped the switch on the wall and changed the soap to water. He began to hose down the truck, rinsing the white foam off. Bob stood by expectantly. Finally Jake turned to him. "What?" he demanded.

"Well—are you?"

"Am I what?"

"Serious about her."

"What are you—her father or something?"

"I'm *not* her father, but I am *your* friend." His attitude shifted. "So I just wanted to remind you of where you are."

Jake cut the water off, then faced Bob again, all without saying a word.

"If you're falling for Sally, I'll be your best man

and break out the champagne. If you think you're going to have a fling, then I'm here to tell you it don't work that way. Not in Comfort.''

Jake's stare was steady. "I know how to treat a woman, Bob.''

"I know you do, and it's not my intention to tell you otherwise. All I'm saying is people are already talking. They've got the two of you behind a white picket fence with babies in the backyard. Sally Anne may think she wants out of Comfort, but you need to remember, she grew up here and she's lived here almost all her life. If other people are thinking that, you can bet it's crossed her mind, too.'' Bob took off his glasses and stared at Jake. "I think you should know her daddy came to see me yesterday. He asked me some questions—about you. What does that say?''

Stunned, Jake shook his head. "Damn! What'd he ask?''

"The usual—where you came from, what you're doing here. How long you plan on staying…that kind of stuff.'' Bob took off his hat and hit it once against his thigh before putting it back on his head. "Look, here, bud, I don't want to see you get in over your head so I dropped by to tell you what's going on. That's all. You're a grown man and you can make your own mistakes.''

8

"I WANT TO KNOW more about M&M."

Sally glanced quizzically through the glass of the booth toward Linda. Linda shook her head in obvious confusion as well. Sally spoke into the mike. "M&Ms? You mean like the candy?"

"No, no. You know, like tying up people and whipping 'em and stuff. I saw this movie the other night and they talked about M&M all the time. What's that stand for, anyhow?"

Sally's forehead cleared, and Linda dissolved into giggles. Sally couldn't hear her, of course, but she could see her friend's face as it turned red and she started to shake. Sally managed to hold her own laughter back. She'd gotten really good at that.

"I think you're talking about S&M," Sally answered. "That stands for sadism and masochism. These are two sexual practices some people enjoy which involve the giving of pain—sadism—or the acceptance of pain—masochism. The partners may use a lot of different aids. As you mentioned, sometimes whips are involved and frequently bondage is

employed as well." *Are you listening, Mom?*
"Does that answer your question, caller?"

"Yeah, I guess. But one last thing…this domi-
natrix woman. What's she got to do with it all?
Dish out pain?"

Sally grinned. "The job of a domimatrix is to
administer whatever the client wants, but yes, that's
what she basically does—dish out pain."

"Well, hell's bells, I think I've found a new pro-
fession for my wife! Thanks a bunch!"

Sally cued in the ending commercial. Who would
think in little ol' Comfort, people would have questions like that? She leaned back in her chair and
shook her head. You never knew what was going
on behind all those closed doors.

She left the station an hour later, exhausted and
wrung out. Doing the show took much more out of
her than she'd ever expected, and the letters that
had started to arrive every day, rain or shine, didn't
help things. They were usually written with crayons
but sometimes in lipstick, which Sally was pretty
sure was Passionate Papaya by Merle Norman. The
notes were hateful and ugly, but harmless. Sally had
gotten to the point where she just sent them, unread,
over to Bob. There had been no more rocks or
slashed tires, so if the letter writing kept the unhappy listener busy, that was great. Today,
though—for a switch—she'd gotten a box of

Godiva chocolates and a fan letter. The glowing compliments had made her feel great. Obviously, not everyone agreed the show was the sure way to hell. Sally had chosen the biggest, fattest chocolate in the box, one decorated carefully with pink sugared flowers and tiny green leaves. She'd left the rest of the candy on her desk, knowing that by the time she came back in the morning, the gold foil container would be long empty—temptation removed.

She paused by the front door before stepping outside and scanned the parking lot. There were no people, just cars, and she felt a tiny spark of disappointment. Jake had been waiting for her almost every day, and she'd come to expect it. He must have had something else to do, she told herself, something more important than sharing a hamburger with her at the Dairy Queen. After their dinner in Medina, they'd kept their evenings simple, but each one had ended the same way, with growing kisses and tight embraces.

It was only a matter of time, she thought, crossing the parking lot. Only a matter of time. Then she'd let him into her bed and what had been inevitable from the very beginning would take place. Jake would make love to her. She'd make love to him. Then they'd come to that awful crossroads a relationship always faced afterward. To keep going or stop. To take it to a different level, or forget about it.

She opened the door to her car, freeing a blast of furnace-like air. Standing there for a moment, she argued with herself. *It doesn't have to be that way! Remember what Jake said? Sometimes a kiss is just a kiss....*

If that was true, then couldn't sex be just sex?

She climbed inside the car and the hot leather seat sizzled against her nylons. Served her right, she thought. She ought to be paying attention, not thinking about sex with Jake. Hell, she'd just talked about S.E.X. for more than an hour with a bunch of total strangers. Wasn't that enough for her?

She answered yes, but was apparently lying to herself. Thoughts of Jake filled her mind as she drove home—Jake coming out of the lake, his long, bronzed legs sturdy and streaming with water. Jake without his shirt, sitting inside his pickup, steaming up the windows. And that first night, when he'd stepped into her house, a stranger, and she hadn't been able to take her eyes off him.

Suddenly, the lights of an approaching car focused her attention on the road. It was going fast, eighty, maybe ninety miles an hour, then all at once it swerved into her lane. She yelled and slammed on her brakes, jerking the wheel at the same time.

The rest was a blur. The other vehicle screamed

by, and Sally got one quick glance. A passing face—white and scared—but nothing more. A second later, Sally lost control and found herself blinded by towering stalks, bouncing through Ed Yasik's cornfield.

JAKE HEARD Bob's cruiser before he saw it. The siren was blaring like all hell had broken loose. He couldn't imagine what would necessitate the piercing wail, but it immediately made him uneasy. He was standing on the porch, waiting, when the car slid up in front of the house and rocked to an unsteady stop.

Bob opened his door and stepped outside the car. "C'mon. We got somewhere to go."

Jake didn't ask any questions. He sprinted to the car and barely made it inside before Bob was fishtailing out of the driveway and heading back down the lane.

"What the hell's going on?" Jake asked, gripping the door handle and looking over at his friend. "The local bank been robbed or something?"

"Or something," Bob answered grimly, throwing him a sideways glance. "Sally Anne just got run off the road. Some yahoo forced her car into Ed Yasik's cornfield."

At Bob's words, Jake's stomach took a bounce and fell to his feet. He'd never experienced this particular sensation before so he wasn't quite sure how to handle it. Throwing up seemed most likely. "Is she—"

"She's fine, she's fine, but her car's banged up and she's scared out of her wits."

Jake's stomach righted itself, but the sick feeling didn't leave. A sweep of anger joined it. "Who in the hell hit her? Was it an accident? Did they stop? Are you—"

"They didn't actually hit her, but beyond that, you know what I know, Jake. I was already home when she called the station. Dispatch called me and I headed straight out. Only stopped to get you first. We'll be there in ten minutes and you can ask her yourself."

They were there in five, Bob slamming on the brakes in front of a white frame farmhouse, a cloud of dust accompanying their stop. Jake jumped out of the cruiser before Bob could even kill the engine.

The screen door squeaked open and a pudgy man in a tan jumpsuit came out onto the porch. He had on a John Deere cap and the right side of his face looked as though he'd been in a prize fight, a knot the size of a golf ball distorting his jaw. He spit off the side of the railing, and Jake realized a wad of tobacco was responsible for the man's appearance.

"Where is she?" Jake demanded.

"Where's who?" the man responded laconically.

"Sally Beaumont."

"Who're you?" was his answer.

Bob reached Jake's side and made the quick introductions. "Ed, this is Jake Nolte, a friend of mine—and of Sally's. Is she inside?"

The man's eyes shifted to Bob. "Yep. The gal's okay. Jes' shook up a little—"

Jake charged past the farmer and pushed through his front door. It took a moment for his eyes to adjust to the dimness. Then things came into focus. He was in a living room, made dark with blinds and drapes. Sally was sitting on the edge of a worn brown sofa while a woman in a faded housedress dabbed carefully at her face. Jake's heart thudded and suddenly he couldn't catch his breath; his chest was as tight as a lug bolt on a tire.

Sally jerked her head up and their gazes locked. Ignoring the protests of her erstwhile nurse, she leaped from the couch just as Jake took two steps toward her. They collided in the center of the tiny room and he wrapped his arms around her. Her body felt frail and shaky and something welled inside him. It was a mixture of anger and disbelief and horror. How could anyone in the world want to harm this incredible woman? He pulled back and looked down into her face.

"Are you all right?"

Her brown eyes warmed to a darker shade of

chocolate. "I am now," she whispered. "But don't turn loose, okay? I—I need you."

"Turning loose of you is not an option," he said roughly. "Don't worry about *that.*"

With his arms around her, Jake led her outside onto the front porch, into the sunshine, and for the first time, he took a good look at her face. She had a small cut over one eye, which he wanted to lean down and kiss, but he held himself back because he knew once he started, he wouldn't want to stop, and Bob was coming up the steps.

Bob reached out to Sally, then dropped his hand when he saw that Jake was holding on to her. "Sally Anne—what the hell happened?"

She shook her head, then winced at the motion. "I'm not too sure. I—I was driving home, minding my own business, when this car just came out of nowhere. I thought it was going to hit me for sure. I was sailing over the ditch and into Ed's field before the damned thing even finished going by."

"The car was coming in the opposite direction?"

"Yes."

"What kind of vehicle was it?" Jake tried to keep his voice even, but it was a struggle with all the emotions fighting inside him. "Did you get the make? The model?"

She shook her head again. "I don't know. It was white—maybe tan. Some kind of pale color. And it was a car, not a truck. I saw the driver's face, but everything happened too quickly. All I saw was white skin, dark hair. I couldn't even tell if it was a man or a woman.''

''Where's your car now?'' Bob pulled out a notebook. ''Do we need to call for the wrecker?''

''It's still in my back forty,'' answered Ed Yasik, who had suddenly emerged from the house. He aimed a brown squirt over the porch railing and spoke from around the gob in his jaw. ''I can pull it out with my tractor. She's scratched up a mite, but she'll start, I reckon.''

Bob nodded. ''Okay—we'll have you do just that, but I want to look at it before it's moved.'' He turned to Sally. ''First, I'll take you over to the hospital.''

''Oh, Bob, I don't need to see a doctor,'' she protested. ''I'm fine, really. It's just a little cut.'' She looked up at Jake, dissolving him with her expression and her words. ''Could you just take me home, Jake?''

He started to object—maybe she *did* need to see a doctor—but she spoke again.

''Please,'' she begged him softly, her eyes filling up. ''I'm okay. I just want to go home. I want to go home and have you hold me.''

WHEN THEY GOT BACK to Sally's place, Jake made a pot of coffee while Sally changed her clothes and cleaned herself up. She followed the tempting aroma of coffee outside to find that he'd already poured her a cup.

She sank to the swing where he sat and they drank their coffee in silence. Jake seemed to understand she didn't want to talk, didn't want to do anything but rest. Finally, he turned to her. It was almost dark on the porch; the sky behind them was streaked with purple and red. She could barely see his eyes, but she could see enough to know they were shining. His voice was gruff.

"It's not too late for me to take you to the hospital. Are you sure you're all right?"

"I'm okay, but I would feel better…" she said slowly, "if you'd put your arms around me and kiss me."

Taking the coffee mug from her hands, he set it down on a nearby table, then turned to face her once more. Very slowly, very tenderly, he put his hands on either side of her face, cradling her. "I can definitely do that," he said. He paused then slowly, he edged his thumb over her bottom lip.

The moment stretched on, then he leaned closer to her and replaced his thumb with his lips. He kissed her so gently that she could barely feel the caress. He pulled back. "Does anything hurt?"

She shook her head. "No."

He nodded once, then angled his head toward hers, kissing her again, still letting his lips barely touch hers. She realized she was going to have to reassure him in a more convincing manner, so Sally put her arms around his neck and pulled him toward her. He hesitated, but she deepened her kiss, edging her tongue into his mouth and moaning against his lips. He seemed to acquiesce and suddenly he was bringing her to him as well, pulling her into his lap as they'd sat in his truck before.

The T-shirt and shorts she'd changed into offered little protection from the heat of his chest and body. Curling against him, Sally could feel his warmth and his interest, as well. She slipped her hand under his shirt and threaded her fingers through the hair on his chest. It was coarse and thick and without thinking about it anymore, she leaned back and pulled his shirt over his head. She wanted to get as close to him as she could. She needed her skin against his. She needed to feel his heartbeat with more than just her hands.

She needed him.

He mimicked her actions, pulling her own shirt off, then leaning back and staring at her in the darkness. She hadn't bothered with a bra and his eyes went slowly down her body, his gaze as hot and compelling as if he were touching her with his hands instead. By the time his look came back to her face, her breath was nowhere to be found and her heart was pounding, fast and furious.

"You're beautiful," he said, his voice husky and deep. "Perfect."

Sally started to shake her head in denial, but she couldn't move. He'd reached out, and with one finger, he was tracing a line around her breasts, first one and then the other. Again his touch was so gentle, so fleeting, it barely registered, yet it left a trail of heated desire she couldn't have ignored if her life had depended on it.

She hadn't imagined the start of their lovemaking to be like this at all. Their previous encounters had been hot—to the flashing point—but now that they both knew the inevitable was about to occur, it seemed as if time had slowed down, almost stopped. Heart-racing desire was building up inside her—and him, too, she was sure—but both of them were overcome by the moment. Through the fog of her wanting, she realized why. She wanted to discover him, slowly and with appreciation. He didn't want to rush, either.

She reached for him, her hands tracing his chest, then pressing flat against the wall of his muscles. Beneath her touch, his skin felt fevered. She brought her face to the place where her fingers rested and began to kiss him, her mouth planting a crooked line up and down his chest to his shoulders and lower. He smelled clean and soapy and she wanted to get so close to him that she wouldn't be able to tell where he began and she stopped.

He groaned, his hands now on her breasts, spreading over their fullness. Could he tell how hard she was breathing? How fast her heart was pounding? She knew he could, but she didn't care. She didn't care about anything except getting closer to him.

He spoke against her mouth. "Do you want to go inside?"

"I—I have blinds," she managed to get out. "I put them up after you showed me the house from across the lake."

"Pull them," he said.

She tore herself from his embrace and reached over the swing to the wall behind them. Unwrapping a cord from around a bracket, she let the platted blind unravel. It fell down with a clatter, enveloping them in sudden privacy and even less light than before. She turned back to Jake and smiled.

He smiled back, but his expression changed quickly—a yearning intensity replacing everything else. Standing up beside her, he pulled her to him and began to kiss her, his tongue pressing into her mouth, his fingers going to the waistband of her shorts. She helped him. The rasp of her zipper was loud in the silence of the dusk, then the sound of his own echoed a few moments later. They squirmed out of their last pieces of the clothing, mouths still pressed against each other's. Sally's need grew to a level she'd never before experienced as they held on to each other, the length of their bodies touching in the darkness.

Her hands roamed over his back and buttocks. Everywhere they touched, her fingers found taut muscle and smooth skin...until she reached around, to the front of his thigh. His scar was slick and polished, a thick line against his skin. She ran her fingers over it.

"Does it bother you?" he asked, moving his lips from her mouth to her neck.

"Of course not," she whispered.

He pulled her even closer, sucking gently at her neck, biting a little bit and sending heated stabs of needy desire to her core.

She groaned in response, her hands moving over his erection to cradle him between her fingers. He sucked in his breath and seemed to hold it as she eased her hands up and down, slowly, provocatively.

"Don't plan on doing that too long." His voice was hoarse.

"I won't," she said, gasping slightly as his fingers eased down her leg to find the juncture of her thighs. "I—I promise."

"That's good," he said, slipping his hand between her legs. "That's really good."

She didn't know if he was referring to her touch or his, but she didn't care, either way. She gave herself up to the feel of his fingers, to the smooth rhythm of his hand against her body, his touch against her core. He seemed to know exactly what she wanted, exactly what she needed and with skillful delight, he brought her to an earth-shattering climax. She fell against him, breathing hard. He took her weight easily—as if it were nothing—and eased them down onto the swing. It moved gently, the ropes creaking, the night breeze easing in between the slats of the blinds, as he pulled her on top of him.

A second later, he was inside her, and once again Sally was lost. The world could have ended at that moment, and she would never have known. Beyond the feel of Jake's warmth inside her, the touch of his hands on her back, there was nothing. There was only Jake.

He gripped her shoulders and his head fell against the bench, the muscles and cords in his neck growing taut and thick as his rhythm built. He cried out her name and a moment later, she cried out his.

9

THEY WERE IN SALLY'S BED when the phone rang the next morning. For a fleeting second, Sally wondered what she'd say if her mother was on the other end, then she looked over into Jake's heavy-lidded eyes.

They'd made love three times in the past twelve hours and she didn't give a big fat flip who knew it. She and Jake could have rolled around on the lawn of the county courthouse and it wouldn't have mattered a bit. He was the most incredible man she'd ever met and a lover unlike any she'd ever had. In between their bouts of wild passion, they'd talked about everything imaginable, including his divorce and the reasons behind it and her near miss with Max.

On the fourth ring, she reached over to pick up the phone, breaking her stare and her thoughts.

Rita's husky voice answered Sally's hello. She spoke with no preliminaries. "You okay?"

Sally sat up slowly. Her body was sore and achy, but she suspected that had more to do with the man beside her than her car accident. "I'm fine," she said. "How'd you hear?"

"Bob told me. I had to call him when I got to the station this morning."

Her voice—and her words—tipped Sally off immediately. "What do you mean—you *had* to call him? What's wrong?"

"We had a problem."

"What kind of problem?"

"You know that box you got yesterday? The one with the candy in it?"

Sally glanced automatically toward her purse. She hadn't had a chance to eat the piece she'd brought with her. The wreck—and then Jake—had robbed her of all thoughts of beautifully decorated chocolates. Which said quite a bit, she thought belatedly. "The Godivas," she said. "I brought one home, but—"

"Oh, my God! You didn't eat it, did you?"

"No…" Sally let the word out slowly, her heart sinking. "Why?"

"Thank God… Ricky found Sonny and Frank in the bathroom this morning, sick as puppies. They came in early and apparently ate the whole box in lieu of their usual donut fest." She took a deep breath. "It wasn't pretty."

"Oh, damn…are they going to be all right?" Before Rita could answer, Jake was sitting up in the bed, his sleepy look gone, every ounce of him focused and leaning forward. The transformation was almost scary. When he motioned to her, Sally put her hand over the phone and quickly explained.

Rita spoke again. "Let's just put it this way... They'll survive, but it's going to be a long time before either of them want chocolate again. I'm not going to give you the details, but I'm so happy that Ricky found them instead of me, I may give him a raise."

Despite herself, Sally started to laugh, but the amusement died quickly. "Ricky found them?"

"That's right."

A buzz started behind her forehead and she blinked twice, her mind going dizzy. "He...he brought that box to my desk and said someone had dropped it off out front. He'd been in reception doing something for Loretta, he said."

The line went silent, then finally Rita spoke slowly. "I think you'd better get down here, Sally. And bring that last piece of chocolate, too. I'll call Bob and get him back up here."

THE SCENT OF Sally's light perfume filled the truck as Jake drove into town. He hadn't noticed it before, but her fragrance was branded into his brain now. He'd smelled it on her skin and in her hair and he'd never forget how it rose from her nape.

He wouldn't be forgetting a lot of things from the night before.

From their previous encounters, he'd thought he'd understood the level of her passion, but last night had proved him wrong. She'd wanted him just as much as he'd wanted her and she'd matched him move for move. There was a freshness in that, he realized now, and it made him feel great. Sandra had always acted as if she was doing him a favor when they'd made love.

He glanced across the seat, an inexplicable emotion hitting him hard. He was feeling things for Sally that he'd never felt for Sandra—and he'd *married* Sandra. What did that mean? He was halfway afraid to voice that question, even inside his mind, but sooner or later, he'd have to face it, wouldn't he? He'd have to face that and a helluva lot more, especially since Sally's one goal in life was to leave town. He'd come to Comfort to kick back, to recoup, not to fall in love....

Her voice broke his reverie. "It doesn't look too bad, does it?" She was gazing into the vanity mirror above her seat, lightly touching the cut above her eye. "I covered it up with makeup."

"You look gorgeous," he said gruffly. "You always look gorgeous."

She reached across the seat and patted his arm. "Right answer, sweetie."

He glanced over at her. "You're a beautiful woman, Sally. Inside and out."

She smiled one of those secret, satisfied smiles that women did sometimes.

"You're damned lucky, too," he continued, his hands tightening on the steering wheel. "Bob's got to get on the stick and figure out what's going on. We can't let this continue."

"Now, Jake—"

"Don't 'now, Jake' me. We need to stop whoever in the hell is behind this vendetta." He paused. "You could have been hurt last night, and who knows what was in that candy?"

"There's one way to fix the situation right now."

"What's that?"

He could feel her looking at him. He turned.

"KFFD in Austin may be making me an offer soon. They've requested tapes and they're interested in the show. This could be my break." She spoke softly. "If I leave, things would go back to normal."

Even though he'd just considered that very thing, Jake's reaction to her words was totally unexpected. When he'd been a kid—twelve or thirteen—he'd caught a helmet in his gut during a practice football game. He felt the same way now. Empty, winded, out of breath and unable to get any more. He covered up the best he could. "You could do that," he said evenly. "But whoever's behind this is breaking the law. They need to be stopped and dealt with, one way or the other."

"But if I'm gone—"

"It doesn't matter. There's a nut out there willing to hurt people." He shook his head, almost to himself. "You've never accepted the seriousness of this, Sally. You always say it's Comfort and things like this just don't happen here." He glanced toward her. "How bad does it have to get before you understand the situation?"

She didn't answer him and they spent the rest of the ride in an uneasy silence.

Bob met them outside. Sally said hello to him then went inside the station, her manner as remote to him as it had been to Jake. He tried to explain, but Bob just shook his head.

"C'mon, Jake, let's face it—the situation's not good, but I don't think Sally's in any serious danger."

Jake exploded. "What the hell do you mean? She's had a rock through her window, her tires slashed, she's been run off the road and now she's gotten poisoned candy. And you don't think it's serious?"

Bob looked at him with a puzzled eye. "Jake— that car was nowhere near hitting her. I looked at the skid marks myself. Sally panicked and that's why she went off the road. If the driver of that car had wanted to really hurt her, they would have waited till she went around the corner. She would have ended up in Dead Man's Creek—not Ed's cornfield. They were trying to scare her, that's all.'' He shook his head. ''And the candy wasn't poisoned.''

''What do you mean?''

Bob grinned. ''That wasn't Godiva in that box, Jake. Beneath that fancy decorating job, there was chocolate-covered Ex-Lax. I don't think anyone's ever died from that.''

Jake stared at his friend in disbelief. ''Ex-Lax?''

''That's right.''

The two men held back their laughter for as long as they could, but it erupted anyway. When they got themselves back under control, Bob spoke again, wiping one eye.

''Listen—I know you're concerned about Sally and I understand, but I'm taking care of things.''

''Not from where I stand.''

Bob stared at him patiently. ''I have Billy Ray drive by Sally's house three times a night, Jake. And once every hour or so, I call Rita while she's here at the station. I'm watching out for her, but this isn't Houston. Someone's just trying to make Sally's life tough. They aren't out to kill her.'' He patted his friend on the shoulder. "Let me do my job, Jake. You're retired now, remember?"

"Is IT TRUE you'll go blind if you…you know…"

The voice was young and squeaky, but filled with concern. Unfortunately, Sally was listening with only half an ear, her mind still on Jake and all they'd shared. She knew he thought she was mad because of what he'd said, but in fact, that had nothing to do with her quietness in the car. She was scared of what was happening between them. What was she going to do? Her feelings for Jake were almost overpowering, but it'd been her dream forever to leave Comfort.

Why now, her brain screamed. *Why now?*

At Sally's silence, the youngster's voice went up, desperation edging in. "You know what I'm talking about, don't you? If you stroke the puppy? Choke your chicken? Slap your monkey?"

Linda's frantic motions outside the booth finally caught Sally's attention. She jerked the mike toward her, horror finally coming over her. "You're abusing animals for sexual pleasure?"

"Arrhhhhhggh… Hellloooo? I'm talking about masturbating, okay?"

Sally's brain clicked. "Oh…oh, yes. I got it. I got it now."

"Well?" A pause filled the air time. "Will I go blind?"

"No. You will not go blind if you masturbate. That's a myth."

"Well, thank you. Finally!"

Sally punched in a tape and spoke over the music. "And now here's a message from our friends down at the feed store. Remember, Johnny carries food for all kinds of animals—puppies, chickens, monkeys…" The ad began and she leaned back, a prayer coming to her lips. "Oh, please, God. Don't let KFFD be listening today…please God?"

THE SUN WAS a huge ball of orange slipping behind the oaks across the street when Sally walked out of the station that evening and saw Jake. Her heart did a funny tumble, then began to race, and as she walked toward him, she could actually feel his stare. His eyes had an almost mesmerizing pull to them, and as she reached his side, she knew that before the night was out, they'd end up in bed again.

He had on his usual jeans and a starched white shirt, and now that she knew the body beneath the clothes, he looked even better than the first time she'd seen him. She pulled her eyes away and glanced into the back of his truck. Half a dozen grocery sacks filled it, one with a couple of steaks and a bag of salad greens sticking out from the top. Her gaze returned to his when he spoke.

"What do you say we go back to the cabin and get something cooking?"

At his sexy tone, she knew he'd forgotten her remoteness this morning. "I can't cook," she confessed. "You'd starve to death if you had to depend on me in the kitchen."

He grinned, those electric blue eyes sending a arc of desire straight into her heart. "That's not the kind of cooking I'm talking about…"

She took two steps and linked her arm in his, shamelessly batting her eyelashes and forgetting all the reasons she should just walk away. "In that case," she answered, "I'm all yours…"

They pulled into the driveway of Bob's cabin twenty minutes later. Jake carried in the groceries and set the sacks down on the kitchen counter, but that's as far as they got. He reached out for Sally, and she went into his arms, her heart thudding against her ribs as she breathed deeply and took in his now familiar scent.

He put his hand on the back of her head and tilted it gently, until their eyes met and held. "I've been thinking about this all day," he said. "From the minute I dropped you off this morning, until right now, this is all I've wanted. What have you done to me, Sally Beaumont?"

"I didn't mean to do anything—"

"But you have, haven't you?"

She nodded gently. "I think I have…and it's the same thing you've done to me. I—I didn't plan on this happening."

He lowered his head and began to kiss her, his lips pressing hard against hers. Sally lost herself in the feel of his mouth, his tongue insistent and demanding, the slick wetness echoing her own body's response to his touch. She couldn't say no to this man.

After a moment, he bent down and picked her up, then strode from the tiny kitchen toward the back of the house. Sally laid her head against his chest, wrapping her arms around his neck. If it could only be like this all the time, she thought.

He sat her gently at the edge of the bed and kneeled beside her, his hands going to the buttons of her suit. Slowly, one by one, he undid them until the jacket hung open and loose. He spread the jacket open, then undid the black bra she wore underneath.

All at once, she knew this time was going to be different. A thrill of anticipation coursed through her as she understood why. There was a urgency behind his features, a kind of controlled intensity that was almost frightening in its strength. She wondered what was going to happen when he let go.

She didn't have long to think about it. He pulled her to him, almost abruptly, and buried his face against her. He kissed her breasts greedily, then his lips went to her nipples, first on one side and then the other. A second after that, he was pulling on them, rolling the edges between his teeth with a gentle bite that only made her want more.

When she knew she couldn't stand it another minute, he pulled back abruptly, slipping her jacket off at the same time, and tossing it to the bed behind them. Her skirt quickly joined it and she was left, standing by the bed in her panties and heels.

Within seconds, he was naked, too. She pressed her body next to his, the hardness of his chest flattening her breasts as his hands roamed over her back with growing urgency. Cupping the weight of her buttocks, he lifted her off her feet, still in her heels. His hand went under her panties and then traced a line forward. Her pulse thundering, Sally cried out as he found her wetness and began to stroke her.

When she went limp, he released her and she eased down his body, her hands slipping from his shoulders, over his chest to the flatness of his stomach. By the time she was on her knees, she was holding him in her hands, the length of his hardness within her grasp. It was his turn to moan as she leaned closer to him and took him into his mouth.

The feel of him, hard and hot, filled her with satisfaction and when she moved her lips up and down, she knew he was feeling the same. A few seconds later, he pulled her away with a gasp.

They fell to the bed, and she reached out for him, to bring him closer, but instead he shook his head. With his hands pressing her into the bed, he kissed her breasts and then her stomach, making his way down her body, his lips leaving a pulsing path behind them. When he was between her legs, his tongue probing and hot against the very core of her desire, she cried out.

By the time she realized he had stopped, he'd lifted his head, pulled her to the edge of the mattress and was entering her.

She gasped and without even thinking she lifted her legs and wrapped them around his waist to bring him closer. She'd never felt this way before—wanting a man so badly, needing him so much. He thrust against her, his hips hitting hers, the rhythm building into something faster, hotter, deeper than she'd ever felt before.

Sally wanted it to go on forever, but as Jake's tempo increased, something seemed to break inside her, a liquid sensation, then suddenly she climaxed—a deep, shuddering climax that rocked her to her very core. Above her, Jake gave a final push, then he too, moaned in release, her name on his lips as he leaned over and buried his face against her damp, hot neck a second later.

They stayed that way, frozen against each other in a tableau of sated passion. Finally Jake pulled back and looked at her, his weight on his hands on the mattress beside her head. His eyes were heavy-lidded and glazed as he stared down at her.

He spoke slowly, almost reluctantly she thought later. At the time, her mind was still reeling from his touch, from the feel of him within her body, and she didn't hear the emotion in his words. She only heard the words.

"You're a helluva woman, Sally Beaumont."

She stared up at him, dazed, breathless, her chest rising and falling. "Wh-what? What did you say?"

He grinned, a slow, lazy expression that made her senses reel even more dramatically.

"I said you're incredible. I love the way you look right now—your eyes all smudgy, your lips all pouty, your hair messed up. I love the way you smell—like sex and damp sheets—and I even love those bright red high heels you've still got on your feet." He leaned down and kissed her gently, his blue, blue eyes drilling hers. "I think I'm falling in love with you," he said softly. "What in the hell are we going to do about that?"

10

JAKE HAD NEVER SEEN the inside of a radio station before, so when Bob called him up and asked for his help, he readily agreed to meet his friend there. Monday morning, they strode into the reception area together, their boots ringing out as they crossed the lobby to the desk of the clerk. Bob had already explained their mission. He wanted to ask Loretta Smith about the package of candy and Ricky Carter's acceptance of it. Back in the days when they'd been partners, Jake had always been the one who could tell if someone was lying or not. Even though he'd improved on his mind-reading ability, Bob told Jake, he could always stand a second opinion. Jake was more than happy to oblige, but he also wondered if Bob had asked him just to pacify him. Jake had made it more than clear he was getting impatient for some results on Sally's investigation.

Loretta Smith glared at them from across the barrier of her curved desk. She had on a headset and a dark blue dress whose white collar tightly circled her neck. Above the pristine lace, several chins hung.

"I'm telling you the truth," she insisted at Bob's first question. "That candy was sitting right here on my desk when I came back from lunch. Me and Pearl went to the Dairy Queen for chicken salad sandwiches and when we walked in, that gold box was right there." She pointed a red-tipped finger to the edge of the desk.

"Was Ricky here then?"

"No sir, he wasn't. He came up here about five minutes later. I had called and asked him to look at my headset—it was on the fritz—and when he finished, he offered to take the box and the mail back to Sally Anne's desk. It saved me a trip, so I said okey-dokey." She crossed her arms and her chins quivered. "I didn't have nothing to do with that box. I didn't even touch it. No sir."

They asked her a few more questions, but it was obvious she knew nothing about the 'candy.' Stepping away from her desk, Bob looked at Jake. "I swear I don't know what to do about this. My only good suspect was Ricky and he's looking clean."

"Even for the car incident?"

"Especially for that. He drives a red pickup and he was here—still at work—when Sally drove off into that cornfield."

Before they could talk more, Sally's low, sexy

voice filled the reception area and Jake realized her show must have started. Loretta shot out her arm and cut off the sound with a sniff. She saw him looking at her and spoke defiantly. "I don't listen to smut," she sniffed.

Jake looked over at Bob, and the sheriff nodded once. He'd caught the word, too. "Let's go in the back," he said quietly. "I need to see Rita before we leave."

They made their way to the rear of the station, going down a long, narrow hallway. "Her office is this way." Bob spoke over his shoulder, pointing to a door. "You can come or you can wait out here."

Jake didn't hear him because he'd already stopped. The corridor had an interior window where visitors could watch the disc jockeys doing their show. Sally hadn't seen him, but he had a clear view of her.

Her cheeks were animated and flushed, the headphones on her ears looking big and awkward over the smooth cap of her hair. Her brown eyes sparkled with interest as she took her first call, and he couldn't stop the twist of emotion he felt as he watched her and listened to her voice over the speakers. It was obvious how much she loved her job.

"Go ahead, caller. What's your question this morning?"

"Well…it's not exactly about sex. Is that okay?"

"That's all right," Sally answered. "We're having an open forum today. Anything goes…"

"Well, in a way, it's kinda about sex, I guess. It's about my boyfriend. We've been dating for almost three months and we have a terrific sex life, but… Well, I think I love him, but I'm just not sure. How do you tell? How do you know when you're really in love and not just 'in lust?'"

Sally bit one corner of her bottom lip, then pulled the mike closer to her. "You've asked a tough question, caller. That's so personal, you almost have to decide on your own."

"Can't you give me a hint?" The woman's voice pleaded, an edge of despair coming into it. "He wants to move in with me, and I'm just not sure."

"Then that should tell you something, right there."

"Wh-what do you mean?"

"If you're not sure, you're not sure. Love hits you hard and if you have to think about it, then maybe it isn't love."

"But what if I'm wrong? I don't want to make a mistake. What if he's the one and I let him go?"

The words seemed to startle Sally, but she recouped fast and never missed a beat. If Jake hadn't been watching her, he would never have known.

"If he's the one, you know. Deep down inside." She closed her eyes. "You aren't able to concentrate on anything but him. When you aren't together, you want to be, and when you are, the rest of the world doesn't even exist. Your stomach stays in knots and nothing matters but his touch, his smile…his voice. You know, believe me. You know."

Then she opened her eyes. And that's when she saw him. There were two panes of glass and fifteen feet separating them, but Jake felt as if she'd reached out and grabbed him. He could suddenly smell her perfume, taste her skin, feel her hair.

And he knew she was talking about him.

Without thinking, he opened the door leading into the outer room. The blond woman inside sent him a startled glance, but he strode right past her and into Sally's soundproof booth. Just before he swept her into his arms, she hit a red button on the console and an ad began to play.

"Johnny's LP and Feed now has everything you need for your summertime pest control…"

But neither of them were listening. Crushing her into an embrace, Jake lowered his head and began to kiss her, the power of their emotions too strong to deny any longer.

JAKE WAITED in the hall while Sally wrapped up the show. She wasn't sure what she had said to anyone who called, including the one guy who wanted to know if you could overdose on Viagra. He was about to go on his honeymoon and wanted to be prepared.

All she knew was that she loved Jake and he felt the same way. They'd told each other so right after he'd kissed her and just as the Johnny's LP & Feed spot had ended. They'd told each other, and everyone else in Comfort. Their words had been broadcast, Linda jumping up and down frantically pointing to the 'On Air' sign. Sally hadn't really cared, though. What she'd told the caller was the truth. She did love Jake—now she just had to decide what to do about it.

Walking down to her office a minute later, she was still grinning. ''Let me get my purse and then we'll leave,'' she said, smiling at him with what she knew was a goofy expression.

He smiled back. ''I'll wait right here.''

She dashed into her office and grabbed her purse, but just as she made it round her desk and to the door, her phone rang. It was Rita. ''Come to my office.''

There was nothing else she could do. Sally went into the hall where Jake still stood. ''My boss wants to see me. There's probably some remote FTC law

I don't know about that says you can't declare love over the airwaves. Can you wait a little longer?''

He leaned down and gave her a look that weakened her knees, his blue eyes staring all the way into her soul. ''I've got all the time in the world. I'll be right here.''

With his hands gripping her arms, he kissed her deeply, his mouth covering hers for one, long pulsepounding second. When he finally released her, she had to stand still for a moment and catch her equilibrium. She felt like she had the time she'd jumped off the Ferris wheel too soon at the county fair.

''I—I'll be right back.''

He nodded and she tottered down the hallway, his eyes on her back. She knew because she stopped twice to look over her shoulder at him as she approached Rita's office.

The door opened just as she reached for the doorknob. Bob stood on the other side, and he grinned at her as she passed him. ''Nice finish to the show,'' he teased. ''I didn't realize you cared about your listeners that much.''

''I love them all,'' she said airily. Turning around she blew Jake a kiss, then disappeared into Rita's office, the warmth of Jake's mouth still lingering on her own.

They loved each other, she thought with a dazed intensity. Nothing else *did* matter. The show probably wouldn't go anywhere, anyway, and if it did, well, they'd cross that bridge when they got there. Nothing mattered right now except loving Jake. That was the only important thing.

"KFFD just called." Rita's voice was excited as it rang out across the office. "They're buying the show!"

Sally's heart stopped. She could actually feel it cease to beat. "Are you kidding?"

"Hell, no! I'm not kidding and neither are they. They want you in Austin by the end of next week." Behind her glasses, Rita's eyes glowed. "It's part of the deal. You have to move there or they won't buy the rights." Grinning, she strode to Sally and held out her hand. "Congratulations, Sally. You've gotten exactly what you've worked for all these years."

JAKE KNEW SOMETHING was wrong the minute Sally walked out of Rita's office. Her face was pale and she wore an expression of shocked disbelief. He hurried down the hall to take her arm.

"What's up?"

She looked at him, her brown eyes two wells of confusion and disbelief. "The show…" she said in a stumbling voice. "It—it's been bought by KFFD in Austin."

"That's…terrific. Isn't it?"

"They want me to move," she answered. "To live there. In Austin."

"Well…great." His throat was so tight he could barely get the words out, but he made his voice strong and filled it with fake enthusiasm. "Isn't that just what you always wanted?"

She blinked at his hearty tone. "Y-yes. It's what I wanted."

"Let's go celebrate. I'll take you by the house and you can change, and we'll go to Medina. Have some steaks."

She nodded slowly. "That sounds wonderful."

He put his arm around her as they went outside. The sun was still beating down with fierce determination. Jake felt the heat, but it barely registered. Inside his chest a ball of frozen denial was building up and taking over. Sure, they'd had a good fling, and sure she'd been fun, but he'd known from the beginning it wouldn't be permanent and that's exactly what they both had wanted. He told himself her moving away would actually work out perfectly—it'd be a natural end to what they'd had and eliminate those messy breakups that always got so bitter.

They made their way to her car, and she handed him her keys without another word. The drive was equally quiet, the silence broken only once when the fire truck of the Comfort Volunteer Fire Department passed them in a blaring hurry.

"Somebody's got trouble," Jake said quietly.

She stared at the red blur as it passed by. "Looks like it."

A moment later, they knew who.

11

SHE SAW THE FLAMES as they turned into her driveway. They were higher than the branches of the pecan tree and licking greedily at her roof. Sally's stomach flipped over in shock. "Oh, my God! It's my house! My house is on fire!"

"Stay calm, now, babe. Stay calm!" Jake wheeled his vehicle around the scattered trucks and cars. "I don't think it's as bad as it looks. It looks like it's just the tree—" Jake threw the truck into Park, but Sally was gone before he could reassure her any more.

She ran toward her driveway where a group of men stood. In the center was Earl Ellis, the president of the Chamber of Commerce and the chief of the tiny volunteer fire squad. He was directing the rest of the men as Sally pushed through.

"Earl, Earl! My God, what happened?"

"Someone driving by saw the flames and called us. It's all under control, Sally. We'll have it out in just a few minutes."

"How'd it start?"

"We don't know yet."

"My house…" she wailed.

He patted her on the arm and spoke soothingly. "It's not that bad, Sally. Really. I think it actually started out there under the tree. It only skipped to the roof because the branches were hanging over the shingles." Turning, he pointed to the edge of her house. "Look—it's already out…the flames are just in the tree. The roof's barely been touched."

Feeling sick, Sally walked closer and inspected the outside brick, her throat tight with anxiety. Earl was right—beyond a smudged window and a little black around the shingles, the place was hardly damaged. The pecan tree would need a serious pruning, though.

"I can't believe it," she said, shaking her head as Jake reached her side. "How could this have happened? I don't understand…"

Earl came toward where she and Jake stood. He held a container in his hand and was looking at it curiously. Smaller than a paint can, it was about eight inches tall and four or five inches in diameter. The label had been burned off. "Sally, is this yours?"

She stared at the container. "I don't know. What is it?"

Jake bent down to look at it better, then straightened, an equally curious expression on his own face. "You didn't throw anything out into the yard last night, did you?"

"Of course not."

Earl shook his head. "Whatever it was, this is where the fire started. Did you have anything outside that was flammable? Paint? Kerosene? Gasoline for the lawn mower maybe?"

Mystified, Sally tore her eyes from the can to scan Earl's face. "No, no. I can't imagine what in the world that could be. I don't store anything that can catch on fire. I'm real careful with stuff like that."

"Well, this can held an accelerant—some kind of fuel." His gaze went to Jake, then to Sally. He spoke gently. "And that tells us something else very important. This fire wasn't an accident, Sally. Someone set it deliberately."

SLEEP WOULDN'T COME, and finally Sally got out of bed at 4:00 a.m. and went outside to sit on the porch. The air still smelled smoky and dense even though the fire had been out for hours. Sipping her coffee, she let her brain wander. Who hated her show so much they'd want to set her house on fire? What was she going to do with the offer from Austin?

Could she really give up Jake and move?

Her thoughts were jumbled and confused and the

harder she tried to work it out, the more complicated they seemed to get. That's why she'd asked
Jake to go home last night. She'd needed to be
alone so she could think about everything.

From behind the house, the sun eased up, the
reflection growing on the lake as Sally sat quietly
and considered all her options. If she left, her
stalker would be thrilled and that problem would
be solved. If she left, she'd accomplish her goal and
get out of Comfort. If she left, her career would
finally take off.

But if she left, she'd never see Jake again.

She'd never had such a dilemma facing her before. Even when she'd come back to Comfort after
college, she'd known what she needed to do and
that had made it simple, even though she hadn't
wanted to come back. Now half of her wanted to
stay and half of her wanted to leave…no, no, that
wasn't exactly right, she thought immediately. *All*
of her wanted to stay and *all* of her wanted to leave.
She wanted Jake and the new job and the peace of
mind leaving would bring her.

She wanted it all.

The lake turned to fire as the sun rose higher in
the sky. Somewhere behind her, on the roof or
maybe in the blackened pecan tree, a mockingbird
cried out, his call loud and strident in the early-
morning stillness. Sally sat quietly and listened to

her heart, but the answer never came. Standing up, she made her way into the house to get dressed and go to work.

JAKE WAS UP EARLY, his usual morning run stretching to eight miles instead of four, his feet pounding the shell driveway, then slapping against the asphalt of the road leading from Bob's cabin. He pressed his brain to turn to something besides Sally, and the first topic it came to was the fire. He and Bob had had a long telephone conversation about it last night and Bob had played the dispatcher's tape while they'd talked. Whoever had called the fire department had been upset and scared...obviously not just a passerby and most probably the one who'd actually set the fire, a not unusual circumstance. The flames had gotten out of hand, reaching for the roof, and they'd suddenly become afraid.

The caller had been a woman.

She'd tried to disguise her voice and to some extent had been successful. Bob had no idea who she could be, but again, both of them had agreed it wasn't Loretta Smith. The receptionist had a distinctive tone, high-pitched and whiny. The caller's voice had been slower, more Southern, even though she'd tried to cover up the accent.

A growing suspicion had been bothering Jake for some time, but he'd put it aside after talking to Bob a few weeks prior. His friend had assured him he was way, way off base, but just to make sure Bob had gone and talked to the person in question. She'd denied everything, of course, and Bob had believed her.

But Jake wasn't sure *he* did.

And that's why he'd asked Earl Ellis for a favor. Earl had looked at him with questions in his eyes, but after Jake had explained, Earl had been happy to oblige. He'd given Jake the can found in Sally's yard and in a few days, they'd all have some answers.

Wiping his brow, Jake forced himself down another turn. They'd have *some* answers, but not the one he really wanted. He'd have to wait on Sally for that one.

SALLY CALLED JAKE on Friday afternoon and asked him to come over for dinner. They'd seen each other only briefly since the fire and the announcement by Rita, and Sally missed him like crazy. If she would be leaving soon, it just didn't seem fair to keep seeing him. It was torture, though. Every night in bed, she would toss and turn and reach out for him only to wake and realize he wasn't there. Did she want to spend the rest of her life wishing for someone who was nowhere near?

She changed clothes three times before he pulled

his truck into the driveway. Wearing a haltered sundress and a pair of white sandals, she met him at the door that evening.

His eyes darkened as he got closer to the porch and saw her waiting. He didn't say anything at all. He simply reached out for her and she moved into his embrace, tucking her head underneath his chin. His arms went around her and held her tight. She laid her head on his chest and listened to his heart beat. It sounded steady and calm—unlike her own, which was pounding wildly.

She finally looked up at him and started to speak, but he shook his head and stopped her, leaning down instead to kiss her. His lips were as demanding and insistent as ever, and she gave in to the sensation, losing herself without thought. They broke apart a moment later.

"I missed you," he said quietly.

"I—I missed you, too."

He didn't beat around the bush. "Are you leaving?"

Her throat closed up. "C-can we talk about that later?"

He looked as though he wanted to say no, but he nodded and followed her inside the house. They stopped in the kitchen to grab two cold beers, then went outside to the back porch. She already had the coals going for the steaks and they sat down beside the pit, the smoky aroma rising from it reminding her of last week's disaster.

Bob had called and told her Jake was working on a theory regarding the fire. She turned to him now to ask him about it. It seemed easier to talk about that than what she needed to discuss with him.

"Have you found out anything about the fire?"

He leaned back, stretching his legs before him and sipping from his beer. "As a matter of fact, I do have some news," he said, surprising her.

She turned to him eagerly. "Tell me."

"I took the can to Austin and had the DPS boys analyze it. The label was gone, but there was enough residue left inside that they got a pretty good sample." His blue eyes gleamed even bluer in the evening light. "That can had shortening in it, Sally."

She looked at him blankly, not believing what she heard. "Shortening? You mean the stuff you cook with?"

"Exactly. Lard, it turns out, is an excellent way to start a mighty hot fire."

"Well, that's weird! Who on earth would start a fire with shortening? I could believe paint thinner or gasoline or something like that, but shortening?"

"How about someone who knows their way

around a kitchen? Someone well known for their cooking skills?''

Sally's mind twirled, then suddenly it stopped and she stared at him in amazement. ''Are you kidding me?''

He nodded once. ''Mary Margaret Henley. It's got to be.''

''No way…''

''Bob is checking out her fingerprints right now. He called her down to the office and took them, then shipped 'em off to Austin. They'll compare her prints to the ones on the notes.''

Stunned, Sally leaned back in her chair. ''God, first the candy, now the shortening…it makes sense, I guess, but why?''

''You can ask her yourself on Monday if the prints match.''

He leaned forward before she could speak again and enveloped her hands in his, his voice taking on a different tone. ''Listen, Sally, I've been thinking a lot about you leaving, and I want to tell you that I think the right thing is for you to leave. We don't have a real future between us, and when we started this, we both knew it. I came here to kick back and you're just starting your life. You'd be a fool not to go.''

The breath left her chest in a whoosh, and no air

came in to replace it. She stared at him and said nothing.

"You've always wanted to get out of Comfort and this is your big opportunity. Hell, if you didn't want to take it, I'd kick you in the butt and make you. Austin's just going to be a stepping stone for you, and you know it."

She took her hands from his and stood up, her chest actually hurting. Until this very moment, she hadn't been sure of what she was going to say. She'd played out all the scenarios—staying, leaving, commuting. In her mind, she'd worked out a dozen different solutions, but this had never been one—Jake telling her to leave.

He stood and came to her side. "This is your chance, Sally. You need to take it."

"But what about us?"

His expression took on a stony resolution. She wasn't too sure what that meant because she'd never seen it on his face before. "What we had was great, but we both knew it wasn't permanent, remember?"

"But I—"

He reached out and put his finger over her lips. The touch was warm and sensual, but he'd stopped her because he knew what she was about to say. That she loved him. That she didn't want to leave him. And he didn't want to hear the words. She wanted to get mad and yell and scream, but she couldn't because she understood exactly what he was doing. It was easier this way. More civilized.

"You have to follow your dream, Sally. If I told you I wanted you to stay here in Comfort and be with me, sooner or later you'd start to resent what you'd given up. The feelings between us would turn into something else, and all the good would go bad."

"I'm not sure I agree."

He took her chin in his hand and lifted her face. "You don't have a choice this time, sweetheart. You're going to go out there and be successful. That's all there is to it."

12

JAKE LEFT as soon as they finished talking, and Sally spent the rest of the night crying. She wasn't at all sure the right decision had been made, but there wasn't anything else she could do. Jake was adamant, and deep down, she knew he'd spoken the truth, at least partially. She would come to resent what she'd given up—but she couldn't help wonder if she wasn't giving up something even greater by leaving him.

She went into Rita's office Monday morning looking like hell.

"I'm taking the KFFD offer." Sally spoke quickly; she didn't want a chance to say anything different from what she'd decided upon. "Call 'em up and tell 'em I'll be there Friday. I want to do one more show here and then I'll go."

Rita's expression didn't hold the burst of excitement Sally had thought it would. In fact, she looked downright upset. "Are you sure, Sally?"

"Why does everyone keep asking me that?" she cried. "Of course, I'm sure. I wouldn't have said it if I wasn't sure. I think things out, remember? It's me, Sally, the analyzer.''

Rita stared at her without saying a word.

''I'm sure!'' Sally insisted. ''Leaving Comfort is what I've always wanted. It'll boost my career. It's the right thing to do.''

''And what about Jake?''

''What about him?''

''Have you discussed this with him?''

''I have his blessing.'' Sally's voice was bitter and the tone surprised her.

''You broke up?''

''There wasn't anything to 'break.' According to him, we didn't have a real relationship anyway.''

''Maybe he just wanted you to go and not feel guilty.''

Sally shook her head. ''We talked about it, Rita. He told me to leave…and he's right. I—I need to go. I *want* to go. Comfort's not so comfortable anymore.''

''All right, then.'' Stepping briskly to her desk, Rita propped her glasses back on her nose and started jotting something down on a pad. ''I'll call KFFD and give them the news. Then I'll call KPDC in San Antonio and tell them, too.''

Sally had already started toward the door, but she stopped abruptly. ''KPDC in San Antonio? Why would you call them?''

Rita continued to write. "They made an offer, too." Finally she looked up. "Didn't I mention that?"

For some strange reason, Sally's pulse jumped. "N-no. You didn't say a word about it."

"Oh, I'm sorry." Rita pulled off her glasses and stared across the room. "KPDC heard your last broadcast and loved it. They called on Friday and made us an offer, too."

Sally waited, but Rita said nothing else. "Well? What was it?"

"Oh, you know...basically the same thing. They want to buy the broadcast and air it in their market. Promote you down there, expand the scope a little. Same thing, except for one minor detail."

"And that was?"

"They said you could record from here and just come into town to do promos. In fact, they insisted on you staying here in Comfort. They said the callers wouldn't be the same if they came from their market. Something about the questions being not as 'quaint.'"

Ten seconds ticked by, then ten more. Sally simply stared at the woman behind the desk. Finally she found her voice. "They said I could do the show...from here?"

Rita nodded. "Yes, but I told them you weren't

interested in that. I told them you wanted to leave—''

Her feet came unglued from the carpet where she'd been standing and Sally bounded across the office. She gripped the edge of Rita's desk for support. ''Call them back!'' she cried. ''Call them back right now. I don't want to leave Comfort. I want to stay here,'' she wailed. ''That's exactly what I want to do....''

Rita grinned and Sally suddenly realized what was going on. Dropping her glasses, Rita pressed a button on her phone and spoke. ''Tiffany, did you place that call I told you to?''

''They're on line three,'' the secretary said. ''I told them you said it was going to be a while, but the guy insisted on holding. Said it was important and he'd wait.''

Rita looked up at Sally and spoke. ''Put him through now,'' she said. ''I think we're ready to talk turkey.''

MARY MARGARET HENLEY glared across Bob's desk. Part of her evil eye was for Bob, but most of it was directed in Jake's general vicinity. Her bright blue eye shadow added a certain emphasis to the threat.

''She made me a promise,'' she said, her Southern drawl more pronounced than ever. ''Sally Anne *tole* me I'd be a radio star, but when that first filthy question came in, I wasn't about to sit thare and be humiliated.''

Humiliated had more syllables in it than Jake could count.

"You didn't think you could work something out?" Bob asked mildly.

"Like what?" she said indignantly. "I don't answer to smut!"

Her lips quivered, and Jake recognized their piled-on color. It was the same shade of lipstick she'd used to write some of the notes.

"Well, Mary Margaret, I got to do something about this, now. I can't have you going around throwing rocks, and slicing up tires and setting people's trees on fire. Not to mention the candy and the car wreck."

"I wasn't even in her lane," she sniffed. "I pulled back way ahead of time. I wouldn't want to hurt my Cadillac! And I called the dad-blamed fire department as soon as I lit that can of shortening."

"And the candy?"

She smiled and patted her hair. "I did decorate that nicely, didn't I? If those two boys hadn't been so danged greedy they wouldn't have gotten sick. I wasn't trying to kill her, for goodness' sake! I just wanted to teach her a lesson, that's all."

"Well, what you did was against the law. I'm

going to have to charge you with malicious mischief at the very least.''

Her blue-rimmed eyes widened. "Am I going to jail?"

"That'll depend on the judge."

"I cain't go to jail. I've got two weddings and a baby shower to cook for next week."

Bob glanced in Jake's direction, barely holding back a grin. "Well, I guess we'll just have to see how things work out, then…"

Bob shook his head and laughed as the unhappy woman drove off a few minutes later in a dusty cloud, her white Caddy almost obscured. "Can you believe her?" he asked Jake. Rising from his chair, he pumped Jake's hand and grinned. "That was damn good detective work, Nolte! I have to say, she had me fooled. I'm glad you caught the cooking grease thing."

"Yeah, yeah…" Jake conceded glumly. "I'm only glad I was able to help."

Bob looked at him with an understanding gleam in his eye. "Too bad you can't resolve your love life as easily, huh?"

Jake looked up. "Is it that obvious?"

"'Fraid so, partner. You better do something fast, or you're going to bleed to death from that broken heart."

"There's nothing I *can* do. Sally's leaving town

for a better job, and I'm not going to be the one to hold her back.''

"Why the hell not?"

Jake looked at his friend in disbelief. "I can't keep her from doing what she's always wanted! She'd hate me for it!"

Bob shook his head. "You may be a damn good detective, but you are one dumb son-of-a-bitch, Nolte. Go find Sally Anne right now and tell her you don't want her to leave. The two of you can work it out somehow.''

"How?"

"Well, damn, it beats me, but if you don't try, you'll always regret it, that much I *do* know.'' Picking up his cowboy hat from the rack by the door, he waved it in Jake's face. "Just leave and go on down to the station. You'll think of something when you get there.''

SALLY TRIED to call Jake five times, but no one answered out at the cabin. She wanted to hop in her car and track him down to give him the news, but with the show starting in five minutes, she couldn't. She barely had time to race into the booth, put on the headphones and take the first call.

"Good morning, Comfort," she said, somewhat breathlessly. "Today's topic is—" She looked up from the sheet of paper in her hand with a chagrined expression. Linda shrugged her shoulders as if to say it was the best she could do. "—um, today's topic is 'Having Sex in Strange Places—Is It Okay?' Call us up and tell us about the most unusual place you've ever had sex." She reached out, her finger hovering over the red button. "First off, though, here's a word from our newest sponsor, Jitters Coffee Shop. Need a pickup before the big date? Trying to keep awake if you've hooked up with a bore? Stop by Jitters and they'll have you jumping in a minute…"

The jingle segued in and Sally hit her 'mute' button. "Who in the heck came up with this topic?"

Linda just grinned. "Hey, I'm doing the best I can, all right? You've been a little busy with poisoned chocolate and burning bushes…"

"It wasn't a bush, it was my pecan tree," Sally countered, "and for your information—"

"Back in three, two, one—" Linda pointed and the phones lit up. Sally picked up line one.

"You're on the air, caller. What's on your mind?"

"Sex in strange places." The man's Texas twang was so thick, Sally could barely understand him.

"Okay, caller." She rolled her eyes and pointed an accusatory finger at Linda. "Go ahead. Tell us the strangest place you've ever had sex."

"Well…uh…you sure these calls are anonymous? I don't want nobody knowing about this, ya unnerstand? You don't have that Caller ID shit, do ya?"

Sally reached for the kill button, but she was way too slow. The word made it to the air. She hoped KPDC wasn't listening just yet… "Um, no, caller. We don't have any kind of way to identify you. Go ahead. Where's the strangest place you've ever had sex?"

The man paused long enough to make her think he'd hung up, then he spoke in a rush. "The strangest place I've ever had sex was…" He began to cackle wildly and then hung up, the sound rattling through her ear phones.

For one stunned moment, Sally let the dead air build then she managed to recover. Punching the next phone line, she said, "You're on the air, caller. Do you have a comment?"

"I don't have a comment on today's topic, but I do have a question for you." His voice was sexy and deep, a growl that reached way down inside her.

"Yes…what's your question, caller?"

"I'm wondering what it would take to convince you that I love you and I want you to stay with me. Here in Comfort…"

Sally's mouth went dry as the words registered, then a movement caught her eye. She stared in amazement as Jake's tall form filled the window leading to the hallway. He held a cell phone to one ear and his eyes were trained on hers, pinning her with their intensity. She felt herself begin to melt under the heat.

"Wh—what you mean, caller?"

"I mean I love you, Sally Anne Beaumont, and I couldn't stand it if you left here. So…would you stay here and marry me? It's not a high-paying position, but it's the best counteroffer I can make to the one you've already received."

Her mouth fell open. "Marry you?"

"That's what I said," Jake grumbled. "I know this isn't sticking to the topic of the day, but if you like, I could call back later, after the honeymoon, and we could talk about strange places to have sex then."

"The ho—honeymoon?"

He grinned. "Hey, for a fast-thinking disc jockey, you need to work on your delivery a bit."

"I—I don't know what to s-say," she stuttered.

"Try yes."

She looked at him through the glass, her heart welling up with an emotion too big to contain. He didn't even know about the second offer—had no idea all their problems had been solved—but he was willing to take a chance and try to work it all out! Taking off the headphones, she walked out of the booth and straight into his arms.

He held her tightly, then she looked up into those bright blue eyes. Behind her, Linda was screaming, "Dead air! Dead air!"

Sally ignored her. "What's your question again?"

"Will you marry me?"

She kissed him long and deep, then pulled back and grinned. "Try and stop me," she said.

Modern Romance™
...seduction and
passion guaranteed

Tender Romance™
...love affairs that
last a lifetime

Sensual Romance™
...sassy, sexy and
seductive

Blaze.
...sultry days and
steamy nights

Medical Romance™
...medical drama on
the pulse

Historical Romance™
...rich, vivid and
passionate

MILLS & BOON®

Winner at

2001 **IDEA** INTERNATIONAL
DESIGN
EFFECTIVENESS
AWARDS

MAT5

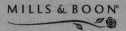

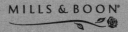

MILLS & BOON®

Modern Romance™

FOR THE BABIES' SAKES by Sara Wood

A heart-wrenching, powerful and dramatic story from Sara Wood – make sure you have a box of tissues at the ready! After catching her handsome husband Dan *in flagrante* with his secretary, Helen discovers she's pregnant with twins. But how can their marriage work if she doesn't trust him?

THE MILLIONAIRE'S AGENDA by Kathryn Ross

From a young author with a contemporary style, this book is just bursting with sensuality and excitement! Millionaire Steven Cavendish enjoyed a purely professional relationship with his PA Chloe Brown – until one night work was forgotten in the heat of passion…

THE LAST MARCHETTI BACHELOR by Teresa Southwick

One red-hot night! Madison did all she could to hide the torch she carried for Luke Marchetti – but their attraction was unavoidable. After one red-hot night, she discovered she was pregnant. Luke was determined to take care of his child *and* Maddie – but she insisted they live platonically. There was no way the excitement Luke felt was platonic!

THE CINDERELLA SOLUTION by Cathy Yardley

Cinderella has a ball! When Charlotte Taylor's best friend, Gabe Donofrio, said she wasn't the type of woman men fall in love with, she bet him a thousand dollars she'd have a marriage proposal in three months! She turned her tomboy self into a sexy siren – and Gabe realised he'd made a big mistake!

On sale 7th June 2002

Available at most branches of WH Smith, Tesco, Martins, Borders, Eason, Sainsbury's and most good paperback bookshops.

0502/01b

MILLS & BOON®

heat *of the* night

LORI FOSTER
GINA WILKINS
VICKI LEWIS THOMPSON

3 SIZZLING SUMMER NOVELS

SANDRA MARTON

raising the stakes

When passion is a gamble...

Available from 19th April 2002

FREE!

2 Books

and a surprise gift!

We would like to take this opportunity to thank you for reading this Mills & Boon® book by offering you the chance to take TWO more specially selected titles from the Modern Romance™ series absolutely FREE! We're also making this offer to introduce you to the benefits of the Reader Service™ —

★ FREE home delivery
★ FREE gifts and competitions
★ FREE monthly Newsletter
★ Books available before they're in the shops
★ Exclusive Reader Service discount

Accepting these FREE books and gift places you under no obligation to buy; you may cancel at any time, even after receiving your free shipment. Simply complete your details below and return the entire page to the address below. **You don't even need a stamp!**

YES! Please send me 2 free Modern Romance books and a surprise gift! I understand that unless you hear from me, I will receive 4 superb new titles every month for just £2.55 each, postage and packing free. I am under no obligation to purchase any books and may cancel my subscription at any time. The free books and gift will be mine to keep in any case. P2ZEB

Ms/Mrs/Miss/Mr..............Initials..............
BLOCK CAPITALS PLEASE
Surname..
Address...
....
....
..............................Postcode..............

Send this whole page to:
UK: The Reader Service, FREEPOST CN81, Croydon, CR9 3WZ
EIRE: The Reader Service, PO Box 4546, Kilcock, County Kildare (stamp required)